So my EX-BOYFRIEND is a SERIAL KILLER

NEW YORK TIMES BESTSELLING AUTHOR

KYLIE SCOTT

Proofreader: Lisa Wolff
Interior Book Design: Champagne Book Design
Cover Design: Elizabeth Turner Stokes

TP ISBN: 978-0-6484574-1-1

PLAYLIST

"Stick Season" by Noah Kahan

"Psycho Killer" by Talking Heads

"The Body Electric" by Hurray for the Riff Raff

"My Doorbell" by The White Stripes

"Bed Chem" by Sabrina Carpenter

"Moonlight in Vermont" by Ella Fitzgerald, Louis Armstrong

"bury a friend" by Billie Eilish

"Saint Elizabeth" by Kaia Kater

"Shake It Out" by Florence + The Machine

"(Don't Fear) The Reaper" by Blue Öyster Cult

"Sweater Weather" by The Neighbourhood

"And Nothing Is Forever" by The Cure

So my EX-BOYFRIEND is a SERIAL KILLER

CHAPTER ONE

MEMORY IS A MONSTER. BUT WE'RE DOING OUR BEST TO use mine for good. Muriel, Hana, and I are having our weekly meeting when the new neighbor arrives. We have a month and a half before we walk the trails with the cadaver dogs and I am determined to have a list of possible burial sites by then. Any new thirst traps entering the neighborhood are just going to have to wait.

"Oh, he's cute," calls out Hana from the front window. She's an Asian American postgrad student with perfect bangs and a pastel aesthetic. "Come and see!"

"What does he look like?" Muriel has white skin, short grey hair, and is a retired librarian. She is amazing.

"Tall with tattoos, dark hair, and a vague air of brooding."

"How can you tell about the brooding?" I ask.

"Oh, that's easy," says Hana. "It's all in the set of the chin."

We work out of the study at the back of my house. Hana calls it the war room. A large map of the local area including nearby national parks is on one wall, and newspaper clippings about missing women are on another. Then there are the photos I took the year I dated my ex. Happy snaps of him smiling at various lookouts. Selfies of the two of us posing beside streams. Ryan loved hiking and getting back to nature. Guess it's why he buried the bodies of his victims out in the wild.

"I don't mind some brooding now and then. How old do you think he is?" asks Muriel.

"I don't know," says Hana. "Thirty or so? Not forty. Somewhere in between."

"They still need too much training at that age," comments Muriel. "Too young for me."

"I actually think he'd be perfect for Sidney."

Muriel snorts. Which is a valid reaction to the idea of me hooking up with anyone.

I raise my head. "Wait a minute. Weren't you just telling me how much dating sucks?"

"That's completely beside the point," says Hana.

Hana and Muriel befriended me nine years ago before the trial. I had already started to keep most people at a safe distance. Cyber sleuths, digital detectives, and armchair investigators have a habit of making my life hell. They either message me demanding information or accuse me of being an accessory and/or psycho killer. But these two women met in an online true crime forum and offered to help me remember all the places my ex had taken me. And they kept offering until I accepted. Because we know Ryan revisited sites where he buried victims' bodies. He once took me for a romantic picnic where the remains of Briana Petersen were later found.

Six women were reported missing during the year he attended a local college. One was later accounted for—she'd been escaping a domestic violence situation. But only one body has been located out of the suspected five. Finding those four missing women and returning them to their families is our goal. Along with proving my ex was guilty of far more than just one case of manslaughter. And I need to do it before he serves out the rest of his fifteen-year sentence. I will not allow him to hurt someone else. No fucking way.

Most of the local police seem to think he's just a boy from a good family who snapped for unknowable reasons and made a single horrific mistake. And most of the general public seem happy to go along with this point of view. But it's bullshit. There is a small online true crime group researching my ex and the missing women. I am not going to sit around and wait for someone to clean up a mess I helped make, however.

"Sidney, come and see," repeats Hana.

I smile and shake my head. It's been almost a decade since I've taken an interest in anyone of any sex. The first time I fell in love was such a disaster I can't be trusted to date. Though I guess just watching wouldn't get me into trouble.

"Why don't you go and take a look?" asks Muriel, who is a secret romantic at heart. But she buries it well. "You never know…he might be the one."

"I'm not sure I believe in the one. Plus I have a lot going on right now. I don't want to get distracted."

Muriel is not convinced. "You've been using that excuse since I met you. It's time you got a life."

"Why don't you go look?" I toss back.

"Because I'm old enough to know better. Now go and ogle the man and make your friend happy."

And I know when I am outnumbered. I join Hana in the living room at the front of the house. "What's going on?"

"He took something inside. At least we're not the only ones

spying." Hana points across the street. "The old couple have been in their garden for ages. And the students in the share house next to them are hanging out on their patio."

Mrs. Lawson, one of my neighbors, is also out walking her dog. The frown on her face when she sees me standing there is mighty. I behave like a grown-ass adult, however, and resist the temptation to hide behind the curtain. It's not easy being the neighborhood pariah.

"What's her problem?" asks Hana.

"She thinks me living here brings down the property values or something."

"We should toilet paper her tree."

"That could be fun."

A man walks out of the house next door. He is indeed tall, with tattoos and longish dark hair. Hana wasn't lying about any of that. And when he grabs a box out of the back of the moving van, the muscles in his arms stretch and strain.

"He is fire," I admit.

Hana happy sighs. "I like it when he lifts heavy things."

"Yeah."

"He doesn't need that place," say Hana. "He can live in my head rent free."

I smile. "That's very generous of you."

"I know, right?"

A young family was renting the small brick bungalow. But they left after someone threw a rock through their window. Doubtless it was meant for me. Maybe Mrs. Lawson was right about those house prices after all.

"I have a life," I say for absolutely no reason.

"Do you though?" Hana wrinkles her nose. "Really?"

"Yes." I laugh. "I do things and see people. Like you two and Mateo and Heather. My friend Salim just stopped by the other day."

"Mateo's your self-defense teacher and Heather's your therapist. You pay them; they don't count. And who's Salim?"

"He's lovely," I say. "He, ah, he brings me things."

"Are you seriously trying to claim the mailperson as your friend?"

I frown. "Maybe."

Hana shakes her head sadly at me.

My life isn't small and pathetic. It just looks that way from certain angles. But what's important is the work we're doing to bring the missing women home. Not the diminutive size of my social life and/or lack of skills regarding same. Most of my friends from high school and college ghosted me. Same goes for the cousin I was close to growing up. I don't blame them, though I did feel abandoned. And me shutting down from the horror of it all wasn't helpful.

There's nothing quite like the social awkwardness of having accidentally dated a serial killer. What my ex did was abhorrent, and he deserves to rot in jail and burn in hell. But my only crimes were being idiotic and in love. Two things that still give me plenty of guilt.

The new neighbor takes another box inside before wandering back out into the sun. And then walking in this general direction. Hana and I jump back from the window in a panic.

"This is it," says Hana. "You're going to meet him."

"*Shit.*"

"What's happening?" Muriel shouts from the study.

Hana yells back, "He's coming over."

"He is? Now this I have to see!"

Thank fuck for thick walls and double glazing. Because my only friends have well and truly forgotten their inside voices. Which is when he knocks on the door.

"I'm not dressed for gentleman callers," I say, giving Hana a nudge. "You like him. You answer it."

"No way. It's your house."

"Yeah, but—"

"Not happening," declares Hana. "I'm doing this for your own good."

It's tempting to wait until he gives up and goes away, which is what I usually do. I don't hate people. But the truth is most of them tend to have a negative opinion of me. The ones in this town, at least. Not to mention my dark blonde hair is overdue for a wash and tied back into a short ponytail. And my white tank top and old baggy blue jeans are clean apart from a small coffee stain from earlier.

A woman needs to be free to be ugly in her own home.

It takes me a minute to deal with the locks on the door, and my twenty-inch baseball bat waits out of sight against the wall. Just in case. Then there he is in black jeans, a faded band tee, and sneakers. He has tattoos on one arm and the side of his neck. And he's both taller and broader up close. I'm average height and weight, and I barely reach his chin. His polite smile warms into something more at the sight of me. Women with oily hair must be his weakness.

"Hey," he says in a deep voice.

Butterflies do not take flight in my belly. It's just gas or something. "Hi."

Hana giggles softly somewhere behind me.

"I, ah, found this in the mailbox. Looks like they delivered it to the wrong house." He hands me a battered envelope. "I just moved in next door. Probably should have led with that."

"Oh. Thanks."

The thing about social niceties is that without practice they fade, and you can go a little feral. Same goes for being attracted to someone without being weird about it, apparently. Because I just stand there staring at the offered limb for a moment. And then for a few more. "Um. Sidney. I'm Sidney."

"Noah." His hand is huge, the fingers scarred and callused. But his grip is gentle. "Nice to meet you."

I'm never washing this hand again.

His eyes are a deep blue beneath thick dark brows. He is without a doubt the prettiest man I've ever seen with those sharp cheekbones and the hard line of his jaw. And I have now been gaping up at him for an awkward amount of time. *Shit.* Which is when I notice the writing on the crumpled envelope in my hand. The way the pen dug deep into the paper. No doubt my ex's thoughts will be gouged into the page in the same way. It's been almost a year since he wrote to me. I wonder what made him think of me now. The ten-year anniversary of his arrest is coming up next month. He always did make a big deal out of birthdays and important dates.

And Noah is still standing there.

The thing is, there's no room in my life for crushes. Not while I have this job to do. This awful history hanging over my head.

"Thanks for delivering this," I say.

Noah nods. "Sure."

Then I shut the door, slide the deadbolt, and hitch the chain.

Storm clouds gather in the night. The wind rushes past the house, tearing leaves from the trees and shaking their limbs. Vermont gets its fair share of weather. I love the drama and noise of it all. The sound of rain on the roof and watching it running down the windowpanes. Though I do miss lying out in the backyard staring at the stars. Some days it's the only time I get outside. You could say I am indoorsy, and you would not be wrong.

My century-old two-story Craftsman cottage moans and groans. But it has good strong bones to weather the storm. I bought it eight years ago with the inheritance after my grandmother passed. The stress of everything that happened was too much for her heart. Yet another death care of my ex.

Staying in my apartment at that point was out of the question. It was too well known. People would pose for pictures on the front doorstep, wait for me to appear and yell questions and/or abusive comments. Then someone added it to an online map for a serial killer–themed road trip and made everything worse. Dark tourism is truly wild. A local tour still operates several times a week that will take you past my old place and to where Briana Petersen was buried. There's money to be made on murder.

Lightning flashes and thunder rolls as the storm passes overhead. Most of the houses on the street sit in darkness since it's the middle of the night. I love it when everyone is asleep, and I have the world to myself. My bedroom is upstairs at the back of the house. A refuge away from everything. I open the side window to watch it all play out and the scent of petrichor is heavy in the air. Though it's hard to see much of what's happening through the boughs of the big old trees.

The letter from Ryan still has me on edge. Science says he has a heart, but what proof do we have really? I might have been raised to be a kind and peaceful person. But it's my dream to one day carve out that supposed heart of his. To put an end to the monster once and for all. A girl can dream.

In the meantime, there are his subtle digs in the letter at how weak and codependent he thinks I am. The painfully polite inquiries about my life. References to the late-night walks I take, the store where I go grocery shopping, and the short length of my hair. He said just enough to let me know he has someone watching me.

Hybristophilia is a sexual interest in or attraction to people who commit crimes. My ex has plenty of fans who write to him and visit. Any one of them would probably be more than happy to keep an eye on me. Taking the letter to the local police isn't an option, though. Some of them still think I was an accessory. I haven't noticed anyone lurking or loitering, but I need to be more careful. More aware of my surroundings.

For now, the security alarm is turned on and everything is fine. That asshole does not get to control me. I refuse to give in to my fear.

Most of the blocks on the street are long and narrow, meaning the buildings are close together. But this house is in its own little world surrounded by maple, pine, birch, and ash. Someone wanted their privacy and planted a whole lot of trees a long time ago. Which is why it's a shame when lightning strikes scarily close and a shockingly loud crack sounds as a huge branch breaks away from the red maple standing directly outside my bedroom. The noise shakes my bones as the limb crashes to the ground.

"Holy shit."

"You can say that again." And staring back at me from the house next door is my new neighbor. We're both standing before open windows in the upstairs levels of our own homes. This is wild. There can't be more than eight feet between us. The tree that got hit is in my yard. He leans out to check the damage and huh. There's a whole lot of skin on display. Biceps and pecs and all that. My heart is not stuck in my throat. It just feels like it is for some reason.

"Are you okay, Sid?" he asks over the noise of the rain.

"Um. Yeah."

"The fence is trashed."

At least my hair has been washed this time. Though my tank and sleep shorts are as old as the hills. It's not like anyone usually sees me before I go to sleep. No idea when I last bought myself something nice to wear. Years most likely.

"Guess you could cut the branch up for firewood," he continues. "I am happy to help if you need someone to do that."

"Thank you. I'll figure something out."

He braces his hands on the bottom window ledge. The way the pose displays his biceps is a thing of beauty. But life experience has taught me not to trust pretty people. The privilege is real. Studies show they are less likely to be found guilty of a crime or tend to get lower sentences. My ex was attractive and look where that got me. I'd been average my whole life. Neither the first nor the last to be selected for sports teams. Just somewhere in the messy middle. Ryan was the first person to really pick me, and it seemed profound at the time. Not so much these days, however.

"Do you think it's a sign?" asks Noah.

"A sign of what?"

"That we're supposed to be friends."

I cock my head. "You think the universe reached out and smited this tree to get us talking?"

"I don't know." He shrugs. "Just seems unlikely that it would be some random natural occurrence. I mean…what are the odds?"

The wind and rain start to ease as the storm moves on. Behind him is a mattress made up with dark linens and a tower of boxes stacked against a wall. We can see straight into each other's bedrooms now.

"I can't exactly tell if you're joking or not," I say. There were nineteen years of normal before my life got derailed. I know how to socialize in theory. It's just been a while since those skills have been put to use.

He smiles. "Let's do proper introductions. Noah Allard. I am thirty-five, divorced, and a chef. A friend opened a restaurant and needed some help, so here I am."

My mouth opens but then closes. I don't want to be curious about him. To be honest, this whole conversation is probably a bad idea. I really can't afford to get distracted from my mission. The cadaver dog trainer has agreed to go out with us for one day in six weeks or so and we need to make the most of it. Last year we searched with ground-penetrating radar. But the moisture level in the soil made it useless. Digging holes here, there, and everywhere in nearby national parks isn't an option.

Then there's the not insignificant fear that my new neighbor doesn't know who I am or my history. When he finds out he might well run for the hills. It's happened before. There's no good time to share a past like mine. Talk about trauma dumping.

And yet.

"What were you going to say?" he asks.

"Where were you before?"

"L.A."

"Big change."

"Yeah. But I was ready to slow down. I needed to," he says. "What about you?"

"I, um, was born here. I'm twenty-nine."

He nods encouragingly. "What do you do for a living?"

"Data coordinator."

"Do you enjoy it?"

"It pays the bills, and I get to work from home."

His smile is lopsided. Imperfect. "You've lived here your whole life?"

"Yeah. In this part of the country. What's the restaurant you're working at like?"

"It's called The Table at the Church Street Marketplace. My friend Ivy opened it a while back."

"What sort of things are on the menu?"

"Starters include steak tartare, oysters on the half shell, and a selection of locally sourced cheeses. For salads we have heirloom tomatoes, cucumber, and burrata, or there's a mix of summer greens with a rhubarb vinaigrette," he recites. "Then I would recommend either the prime striploin with green peppercorn sauce and fingerling potatoes, halibut with crispy brussels sprouts, or wild mushroom rigatoni with parmesan and truffles."

"Wow. What about dessert?"

He grins. "You got a sweet tooth?"

"Let's just say I could definitely do with some sweetening up."

"Flourless chocolate cake, rhubarb crème brûlée, or a house-made honeycomb ice cream sound okay?"

"They sound amazing."

"That's because they are. You should visit. Let me feed you sometime."

I smile and try to be normal.

And apparently fail, because he asks, "But you're not going to, are you? Why is that?"

I am not agoraphobic or anything. The last time I went to a bar with Hana, however, I had to leave. A bartender who knew Briana Petersen saw me and started to cry. Had a breakdown in the middle of happy hour. I don't want to risk retraumatizing someone just because I'd like a beer.

Vermont has my heart. But there's a good chance I am going to move to a city on the other side of the country. Once we find the missing women, of course.

"I don't tend to go out much," I say.

"You're a homebody, huh?"

"Yeah."

"What do you do for fun, Sidney?"

"What do I do for fun?" I raise my brows, search my brain, and come up with absolutely nothing. Not a single damn thing. I mean there's dancing in the kitchen while eating cookies straight out of the wrapper. And there's reading a romance book on the back porch. Which, with or without a bottle of wine, is still a guaranteed good time. But both of those are alone things. I highly doubt they're the sort of activities that a. would impress him and b. he's really asking about. There's a small chance Muriel and Hana were right about me needing to get a life. "That's a good question. I mean…I've heard of the concept. It's just been a while."

He waits.

"I might have to think about it."

He watches me for a moment. Then he glances down at the tangle of tree limbs. "Let me know if I can help you with that, okay?"

"Thanks."

He gives me a last look before he turns out the light. However, he doesn't close the window. And I don't know why, but it feels important.

CHAPTER TWO

A SERIAL KILLER IS GENERALLY DEFINED AS A PERSON who commits a series of three or more murders. They usually operate within a defined geographical area. A comfort zone near their residence or place of employment where they feel confident targeting, capturing, controlling, and disposing of victims. We believe that for Ryan, this was between Burlington and Mount Mansfield. Which is still a vast area to search. But there are limits to how far a person can carry dead weight—how far from wherever he left his car he could bury a body. Matching this information to the places where he took me is the key. Particularly the locations where he liked to linger for a while when we went on hikes.

Therefore, Muriel, Hana, and I spend Saturday in and around Stowe. And what a gloriously sunny, hot, and bug-filled time it turns out to be. Hauling our asses all over the mountain makes for a long day. But over the years we have found a café with the best grilled chicken chopped salad in existence. It helps to alleviate some of the pain—especially when combined with cake. The special today was a vanilla maple whiskey cupcake, and yum.

"Noah's ex-wife is gorgeous. I am obsessed. The separation mustn't have been too bad if he didn't wipe her from his socials. Can you imagine being friends with an ex?" Hana asks as she slouches in the backseat of the Subaru on the way home. She's in charge of the music and we're listening to Paris Paloma. "Well, no. Not you, Sidney."

My smile is as wry as can be.

"Let me see," says Muriel. "My cell's out of batteries or something."

"What have you done to it now?" asks Hana. "Why does technology hate you?"

"I thought I plugged it in, but I guess not," grumbles Muriel.

I hand over mine without taking my eyes off the road. "Here."

It took them hours to get his full name out of me. Though the truth is, I want to talk about my new neighbor. I haven't seen him since the night of the storm due to work. They've had me doing extra hours. By the time I go to bed, the light is out in his bedroom. Muriel finds him on social media in no time. I have not been creeping on him, but he is at the top of my most recent searches. Let's not ask why.

"He was sous chef at a restaurant in West Hollywood with a Michelin star," continues Hana. "Talk about goals."

I nod. "He said he needed to slow down."

"Vermont is certainly a good place to do that," says Muriel.

"So, you have been talking to him." Hana sizes me up in the rearview mirror. "And you didn't say a word. How many other secrets do you have hidden?"

I just laugh.

"This is good news," says Muriel. "You could do with more people in your life."

"You're going to get one of your online contacts to search his credit rating and criminal history, aren't you?" I ask, already knowing the answer.

"No," says Hana archly. "That would be a massive invasion of his privacy."

"Of course we are. You can never be too careful." Muriel peruses the screen. "I didn't realize you were back on social media, Sidney."

"I am not really," I say. "It's a locked account and I didn't use my full name."

"But still…you're putting yourself out there. Albeit in a limited fashion."

"It was my therapist's idea. To embrace some of the activities other people my age are doing."

"You're so cute when you're being all normal," says Hana with a smile.

"Thank you. I used to like taking photos. It's been good getting back to that." I smile. Then I stop smiling. "He asked me what I do for fun."

"Who?" Muriel turns my way. "Noah?"

I nod.

Hana's gaze meets mine in the rearview mirror. "And what did you say?"

"I didn't know what to say," I admit dismally.

Muriel half turns in her seat and shares a pointed look with Hana. There's a small chance I don't like change. Or admitting that my life sort of sucks. But here we are.

"You should ask him if he'd like to be your new hobby," says Hana.

I just smile.

"Or you could ask him out?" Muriel nudges me with her elbow. "It's the sort of thing normal people do sometimes."

"Sidney, we haven't gone out in ages," says Hana. "I've been so busy with school. What've you been doing with yourself outside of this and work?"

"Well…I read and stuff."

The two exchange another look.

"I like my own company," I say. "Being by myself isn't so bad. For instance, I enjoy disassociating and taking long walks."

"Who doesn't?" Hana shrugs. "We should all regularly make space in our lives to be antisocial. But don't you get lonely sometimes?"

I don't know how to answer that question. Nor do I want to.

"It's been almost ten years." Muriel sighs. "I know you don't want to hear it, but there's a chance we may never find their bodies."

My fingers tighten on the steering wheel. "We have to. Then everyone will know exactly what he did and how many people he hurt. Their families will finally have closure."

No one speaks.

"If either of you want to stop, I would understand."

Muriel shakes her head. "No."

"Same," says Hana. "But you getting a hobby is a good idea. Having something in your life other than death and taxes."

"I vote for you knocking boots with your neighbor," suggests Muriel.

Hana laughs.

It's not a bad idea. Not the having-sex-with-Noah part. The bit about me getting a hobby. Bringing the missing women home is my mission, but maybe there's room for more. Maybe. "What if he's only being nice to me because he doesn't know who I am?"

"He might know and not care," says Hana.

"Or he might know and be waiting to form his own opinion." Muriel's gaze stays on the screen. "It makes sense to try and protect yourself after everything that's happened. But you don't want to overdo it."

I am not convinced.

Which is when Muriel stabs at the screen with a finger while asking, "What does this button do?"

"You followed me on social media," says Noah with a smile.

"And you followed me back." There's no way I'm telling him Muriel was responsible. How embarrassing. "On your way to work?"

It's midmorning Wednesday and we're standing in my driveway. He's dressed in a plain white tee, black pants, and matching Birkenstock leather clogs. Which I guess is what chefs wear. I am wearing my old blue jeans, a boxy tee, and a baseball cap. I used to like sundresses and crop tops and such. But now it's all about boring, safe, nondescript clothing to blend with the masses. Not standing too tall in case someone sees me as a threat. Things like that. People still often recognize me. They associate me with the fear and horror they felt back then when more women than normal were disappearing. So long as I avoid eye contact and keep moving everything is usually fine.

"Yeah." He nods to the bags in the back of the small Subaru SUV. "Can I help with those?"

My first instinct is to say no. A good indicator it's the wrong thing to do. I don't want to hide when it comes to him. Maybe Hana and Muriel are right about it being time for my world to get a bit bigger. "Sure."

He steps forward and inspects my grocery purchases. There's no other word for it. But me and my things being perceived by this particular man isn't so bad. His interest doesn't seem prurient like some. Then he gathers up the bulk of the bags in an impressive feat of strength and organization. What a useful person to have around.

"Just at the front door would be great. Thanks."

He nods.

A cop car cruises down the street, but I don't recognize the person behind the wheel. Which is a good thing. "I know you're dying to say something about all of the microwave meals."

"There's nothing wrong with convenience," he says. "I'm more of a frozen pizza guy myself. I actually need to stock up. Where do you recommend getting groceries that's local?"

"I like the co-op."

"Duly noted. Haven't seen you in your bedroom window lately." He stops and blinks. "That sounded sort of perverted and stalkerish, didn't it?"

"Just a little."

"Shit." He deposits the bags by the door. One side of his mouth rises higher than the other and it's charming as fuck. "Sorry 'bout that."

Music is blasting from the student share house. And

the old couple across the road are out working in their garden again. I refuse to worry about whether they're watching or what they're thinking. We're not doing anything wrong. Marigold, daisies, dahlia, and zinnia are in bloom in their yard, making for a riot of color. End of summer is a good time for gardening. My grandmother used to love growing things. She had a theory that gardens should be half pretty and half purposeful. For every tomato plant or cucumber vine there had to be a flower. She was big on balance. Which is not something my life has seen much of lately.

"Are you okay?" he asks.

"Yeah. Just thinking."

"What about?"

"Flowers, weirdly enough."

"Nothing wrong with flowers," he says. "I have to go."

"Thanks for carrying those."

He nods and stands there. Not leaving. Not even a little. And there's this energy between us. This awareness of each other that I haven't felt in forever. Then he asks, "Talk to you later?"

My smile is as wide as can be. "Okay."

"Keep your hands up," says Mateo, throwing another jab at me.

The previous owners used the separate garage for storage and an office. I use it for something else. There's a punching bag for me to practice hitting and kicking. Some hand weights, a skipping rope, mats and such. Mateo teaches mixed martial arts. How to throw a punch, guard myself, and get out of a hold. There's a lot of focus on eyes, throat, groin. He comes over regularly to train me in private. Wednesday night suited him this week.

I started training with him not long after my ex got arrested. Some online forums theorized that I helped him. Others went even farther, claiming that the evidence pointed to me as the killer. Which is the truth. But there's no getting around the fact that I had an airtight alibi. Then came the death threats from strangers. People yelling in my face in front of my apartment. And then some guy grabbed me and shook the shit out of me. His niece had gone missing the year before.

Mateo is about my height with more muscles than I can count, a buzz cut, and olive skin. We're both wearing shin and foot guards, sparring gloves, and mouth guards to spare ourselves from the brunt of the attack. He blocks a particularly devastating roundhouse kick from me. Then says, "That was half-assed."

"Harsh."

"Go again."

I assume the stance—my fighter's kamae. Feet shoulder width apart with my kicking leg at the back. Twist my hips and bring my rear foot forward and straighten the leg.

He grunts as he blocks the hit. "Better. Keep your hands up."

I throw a jab, which he dodges.

"Come on, Sidney. Show me who's boss."

I sway backwards, avoiding an uppercut.

"That's it. Good work."

Now I'm in the zone. Which is when I hear the rumble of an engine coming down the street. For a moment I think it might be Noah returning home early, but then the vehicle drives straight past. This second of lost focus is all it takes. Mateo's right hook really is a thing of beauty. His gloved hand sails through the air and his fist slams into the side of my face, and oof.

"Hey," says Noah as he climbs out of his car.

It's Thursday night and the street is otherwise empty. Midnight is a quiet time when this place becomes a safe space for me to show my face and take a walk. There's usually just me, the streetlights, and neat rows of houses sitting in silence. I didn't account for him arriving home from work so late.

The smile falls off his face as he steps closer. "What the fuck? Sid, who hurt you?"

"It was an accident." I touch my swollen and bruised cheek. "I got distracted during training."

"What sort of training?"

"Self-defense."

"You do boxing or something?"

"Mixed martial arts."

He gives me a long look. "And you're sure it was an accident?"

"Yes. Mateo has been training me for years. He felt awful about it. Though it sort of balances out the time I split his eyebrow, and he had to get it glued."

"What distracted you?"

"I can't remember," lies my lying tongue.

His shoulders ease as the tension leaves his body. Though the frown doesn't totally vacate his face. It lingers in the furrows on his forehead. He peruses my tank, shorts, and sneakers and asks, "You heading out?"

"Going for a walk."

"Alone at this hour of the night?"

"I like the quiet and I'm kind of nocturnal."

"Would you mind if I came with you?"

I open my mouth, but it takes a moment for words to form. It's sweet of him to worry. But I can look after myself. "There's no need to—"

"It's just that I've been stuck in the kitchen all day." And he gives me the smile. The one that hits me straight in the heart and between the hips. Hana performed a litany of online searches and confirmed he shouldn't be a danger to me. But she doesn't know the effect he has on me. This is dangerous. Losing focus and getting punched in the face confirmed as much.

"I have a taser," I say. "And pepper spray."

His brows rise. "I promise to mind my manners."

"No…what I mean is, you don't have to worry about me."

He nods. "Okay."

I wait for him to change his mind or make an excuse and go inside. But none of those things happen. "You still want to come on my walk?"

"I really do."

"Let's go then."

The lake lies to the west of us. I tend to vary my route, but rarely my destination. Walking helps on the nights I need to outpace the past. It reminds me there's a big, beautiful world out there just waiting to be discovered. A dog barks somewhere and soft music can be heard coming from a house in the distance. Noah says nothing. Just walks beside me with his hands stuffed in his pants pockets. I like how he doesn't feel the need to make conversation. I used to be chatty, but now I guess I'm more used to silence. He does, however, keep giving me side eyes and a hint of a smile. It seems companionable or friendly. But my heart of course completely overreacts. Walking with Noah just might be the most exciting thing to happen to me in years.

We cover a couple of blocks and pass the brewery, a coffee shop, dispensary, and pizza place. The only other signs of life are a cat dashing across the road and the occasional car driving past. I feel oddly delicate beside his brawn despite my ample ass. And he's definitely shortened his stride so as not to outpace me. The sleeves of his white work tee are rolled back, showing off his biceps just so. I should probably stop ogling him. That would be good.

We soon clear suburbia and hit the shoreline. The lake is a dark expanse of water beneath a sky full of stars. There are a couple of boats anchored nearby, and a warm breeze is blowing. But otherwise, all of the world is silent and still. Home is for feeling safe and sound. Standing here by the water is for breathing deep and being free.

Noah takes it all in, not talking for a while. Then he clears his throat and says, "This doesn't suck."

"No," I agree. "It doesn't."

"Choosing Vermont as the place to slow down and stress less is working well. And you've lived here your whole life?"

"I grew up on the other side of the city, but...yeah."

He waits for me to continue.

"My, um, grandmother raised me. Then, after she passed, the house was too big for just me. And I was ready for a change of scenery, so I moved to South End."

"No siblings?"

"No," I say. "What about you?"

"Born and raised in Sacramento. My parents and younger sister still live there. She's married to a great girl with a baby on the way."

"You're going to be an uncle. Nice."

He smiles and tips his head back to stare at the sky. "I used to love stargazing when I was a kid. Too much light pollution in L.A. This is a little better, though."

"Which is your favorite constellation?"

He points overhead. "Ursa Major. What about you?"

"Centaurus."

"Some solid stars," he says.

And I am not imagining things when he steps just a little closer. No internal alarms start ringing. Nothing about him makes me nervous in a bad way and sets off my fight-or-flight response. A very good thing. Though it would be great to not overthink it and enjoy the moment. Something which is unlikely to happen, however.

"Tell me about your day," he says.

I think it over. "I spilled coffee on my keyboard for the hundredth time. Kind of amazed it hasn't died on me yet, actually."

"I salute your keyboard's staying power."

"Me too." I smile. "And I came up with an amazing new bagel combo for lunch."

"Tell me."

"Avocado, ham, a fried egg, cream cheese, and a lemon-wit h-cracked-pepper-and-sea-salt spice mix."

"That sounds really good."

"It was some epic comfort food. What's your favorite filling?"

"I am pretty traditional with the cream cheese, thin-sliced red onion, capers, and lots of salmon."

"It's traditional for a reason though, right?" I ask with a smile. "How was your day?"

"Someone used one of my knives. But it was okay."

"You don't like people using your knives?"

"No. I have been known to be weirdly possessive about them. It's not exactly unheard of in the industry. They cost me a lot of money and I look after them well."

"That makes sense. You've got to have the right tools."

He just nods.

"Are you happy you didn't freak out?"

"I really am. Feels like a positive step forward, you know?"

"That's good," I say. "So, your life in L.A. was tense?"

"Yeah. When you find yourself losing your shit five times a night, five nights a week, you know it's time to make a change." The breeze picks up, tousling his thick dark hair. Being here with him is nice. Sharing this with him. "Ever get the feeling that your life isn't turning out how you wanted?"

"Yeah. I, um, I'm familiar with that feeling."

"Success looked different when I was younger. I thought it equaled instant happiness. The high pressure, long hours, endless stress, but good money sort of situation. Working where I did made me a better chef. But it turned me into a miserable fucking human being," he says with a dark laugh. "Which is my way of saying I like this a lot. Being here with you."

"I like it too."

No one has been this open and honest with me in forever.

Not someone I just met. What must it be like to be so willing to take a chance on people getting to know the real you? To be brave and show them all of your faults and flaws?

He takes a deep breath and turns back to the water. "Tell me something else about you."

"Um. Let me think…" I stare out at the water too and think calm thoughts. "I wanted to be a teacher when I was at college."

"You like kids?"

"I did. Yeah. No idea if I would have been any good at it."

"What happened?"

"My life changed…I guess I changed."

"Teaching has to be a damn hard job."

"Right?" I ask. "It must be so challenging with the current political climate and everything. The book banning and lack of funding and the rest of that bullshit. You would have to really want to be there. To really believe in what you're doing."

He nods in agreement.

"I envy people who have a calling. Who just know what they want to do. Is that how you felt about being a chef?"

"No." He laughs. "I just kind of fell into it. A friend of the family owned a restaurant and was after an apprentice. So, I thought why not give it a go. But I was always interested in what was going on in the kitchen. My great-grandmother lived with us for a while when I was little, and she was always cooking. The woman just never stopped. Bread and soups and stews. She grew up in Poland and knew every recipe by heart. Never needed to look up a damn thing. I thought she was amazing."

"That is amazing. I can barely remember how to put a grilled cheese together."

He grins, and how dare he be so gorgeous. Seriously. Shame on the man. "You come here every night?"

"Not always."

"What else do you do?"

We're basically back to the what-do-I-do-for-fun question. I have given it some thought and have a response prepared. "Sometimes I lie in the backyard and stare at the stars. We have that in common. I have a fire pit and…I don't know. I just like hanging out and reading."

"That sounds good too. I haven't looked at anything that wasn't a cookbook in forever. What's the last thing you read that you loved?"

"They were romances. *I'll Come Back for You* by Charish Reid. It's a spooky one. And *Morgue to Love* by Megan Montgomery. The heroine is a medical examiner." Because even my reading tends toward the morbid. There's a small chance I am obsessed with death.

"Interesting," he says, taking a step closer for some reason. He stares down at me and holy shit. I think he's going to kiss me. My stomach flip-flops in the weirdest way. The truth is, I want this so much it hurts. But then he leans in and asks in a low voice, "Do you really have a taser and pepper spray on you?"

"Yes."

"Good," he says. "That's good. Because not to scare you, but I think somebody is following us."

My smile disappears as I turn to face the quiet street. I should have been more aware of my surroundings. There's always an element of danger being out this late at night. I'm not stupid. I know this. Though the benefits have always outweighed the risks for me.

It takes me a minute to find the person standing in the shadows beneath a fir tree in someone's front yard. When she sees me watching, she steps forward into the light to show herself. Long blonde hair falls down over her shoulders just how my ex always liked it.

Noah relaxes at the sight of her. He shouldn't. It's been guesstimated that one in every hundred people are psychopaths. And some of those are definitely female. Women make up a small percentage of serial killers, but they tend to get away with their murders for longer. They're also more likely to be motivated by revenge than their male counterparts. Though profit is also a favored reason for womenfolk. Which doesn't mean there aren't female thrill killers. They just tend to be a bit of a rarity. I doubt homicide is why she's here, however. The bitch is just messing with me—which is confirmed when she turns and walks away without saying a word.

Maybe I should use this moment to explain things to Noah. Take a chance and tell him about my past. Though, let's be honest, my complicated situation and difficult history are hardly going to appeal to someone looking to relax and enjoy life for a while. Ignore my raging hormones. There's a good chance that friends is as much as we'll ever be.

"Strange," says Noah, watching as my stalker walks away.

"Yeah." I breathe deep and say, "We should head back."

We're close to home when a cop car slows down and stops beside us. The way my stomach sinks below street level.

Something like this was bound to happen sooner or later. But this is really not my night. Fuck my life.

"Sidney," says the man in uniform sitting in the vehicle.

"Officer Smith."

He scowls at me, and I stare back as blank as can be. Giving nothing has proven to be the best way to handle these encounters over the years.

"Is something wrong?" asks Noah.

"Just checking to make sure you're okay," says the officer.

I keep my mouth shut.

"She's fine," says Noah.

"Oh, I wasn't asking about her." Officer Smith gives me a look of distaste. "We like to keep an eye on the company she keeps. For safety's sake, you know?"

Noah's brows draw down in confusion.

Shit.

"He doesn't know?" A wide smile splits the officer's face. "Good heavens. You're taking your life into your own hands here, son."

"What is he talking about?" Noah asks me.

My mouth opens, but nothing comes out. Just a whole lot of nothing. I am so cooked.

Officer Smith laughs. "Miss Walsh used to date a convicted felon. A murderer as it so happens. Though they only managed to get him on manslaughter. There are still some who believe she was involved in the disappearance and suspected death of several people. Isn't that right, Sidney?"

Noah just blinks.

Officer Smith smirks as he drives away. Such an asshole.

I swallow hard. My throat is as dry as can be. "I wasn't involved. I didn't know what he was doing."

Noah just stares at me for a second. And I can feel a sudden distance growing between us. A wariness in his gaze. "I'll walk you to your door."

He closes the window and draws the curtains when he goes to bed. And I get the message he's sending, loud and clear.

CHAPTER THREE

A CRASHING SOUND WAKES ME. I BOLT UPRIGHT IN BED at some small, awful hour of the morning. There's the screech of tires as shouting and laughter comes from the street. My fingers fumble for the phone and taser sitting on the bedside table. It's been a while since something like this happened. A few months at least. But my brain goes from sleep addled to wide awake in an instant.

The wooden floor is cool against the soles of my feet as I move out of my bedroom, down the stairs, and to the front door. No more noise is coming from outside. Everything is still and silent. As it should be at almost three a.m. on a Sunday. There's nothing interesting on the security cameras either when I look on my phone. Though I check the front windows, just to be sure. Then I unlock the door to see what's happened this time.

Lights have turned on in a couple of nearby houses. I don't know what drunkards and assholes used to do for fun in this town. But harassing me is apparently a guaranteed good time and has been for years. You can't really blame the neighbors for not liking me.

And there lies the reason for the almighty crash. Where my

mailbox used to be are its smashed remains strewn across the ground. Tire tracks have also chewed up the surrounding grass.

Fuckers.

Noah appears at his front doorstep in a pair of sleep pants and a loose tee. "What is it?"

"Just some idiots being true to their nature."

His gaze is dark in the dim light. "Does this sort of thing happen often?"

"Often enough."

The lights go out in one of the houses across the street. No doubt somebody heading back to bed after checking out the commotion. Which is a damn good idea. The ruins of my mailbox can wait until morning.

I turn to leave. "Night."

"Why do you stay here?" he asks. "If this shit is always happening and people hate you?"

"It's complicated. You looked me up, right?"

His jaw tenses. "Yeah."

"I'm not in the sort of situation that goes well with relaxing and enjoying life."

"No," he agrees with anger in his eyes. "Why didn't you tell me?"

"You didn't seem to want to talk about it the other night. As for before that...my ex is one of the worst things that's happened around here. It's not easy starting introductions with the biggest mistake you ever made being so well known. But it also happened ten years ago, and I'm trying to get on with my life as much as I can. And you and I had only talked a handful of times."

He frowns.

"I like you, Noah. I like to think I would have told you sooner rather than later. But the truth is, I don't know. People don't tend to hang around long after they find out. I guess what I am saying is you're right to be angry, or however you're feeling. Not that you need my permission."

He doesn't say a word.

"There was something between us, wasn't there?"

"Yeah," he answers eventually. The truth is I barely know him, but losing the idea of him hurts. At least, that's what I tell myself as I walk away.

Hana texts me the next morning.

> Hana: Amateur photography group meets at the brewery near you once a month.

> Me: That could be cool.

> Hana: You should go.

> Me: But people.

> Hana: People need to get over themselves and get used to you. Something that's never going to happen if you keep hiding at home.

> Me: Harsh but fair.

> Hana: Ask your neighbor to go with you.

> Me: He found out about me. Wasn't happy.

> Hana: Shitty.

> Me: Yeah.

Hana: Did you know female raccoons are monogamous but males are polygamous?

Me: No. Random but fascinating. No wonder they often seem angry and prone to violence.

Hana: I know, right?

Hana: My point is you can't trust men to make good choices.

Me: So sad.

Hana: Why are men?

Me: We may never know.

Me: When does the photography group meet? Just out of interest…

There's a store on Pine Street I've had my eye on forever. Any time I drive past, I check out the windows. The aesthetic is minimal and modern. Though they stock cute stuff too. Dresses, tops, and bottoms that are feminine without being overly frilly. Other people walk into shops all the time. It shouldn't be a big deal. But I sit in my parked car for half an hour before working up the nerve to enter. Which is ridiculous.

I want my life back, or some semblance of it. Things are never going to be like they were. My grandmother is gone, and certain people think I am a murderer or accessory to the same. Nothing I can do about it. What I can do is stop skulking about the fringes of society like I am actually guilty.

There's a long list of things I used to do. Watch movies and go dancing and hang out with friends. Hana is right about how me hiding at home achieves nothing. My face was everywhere when Ryan was arrested, and all throughout the trial, I tried to respect people's feelings and stay out of sight. But after almost a decade, I seem to have reached my limit for behaving like an outcast and being blamed for something I did not do. Anger at the situation with Noah might also have pushed me into doing this today. Stupid men, stupid hearts, stupid loins, etcetera.

Though some fixing up of my self is long overdue.

I don't notice my stalker until I'm almost at the shop door. She's standing on the other side of the street watching, her long blonde hair shining in the sun. She's wearing a white floaty dress. And she's both younger and thinner than me. I stare at her and she stares at me and ugh. The girl's going to have to try harder if she wants to scare me. No way does she get to ruin my day. I am a grown-ass woman and more than capable of doing that all on my own, thank you very much.

But she and I should chat. There are some questions I want to ask her. I look both ways searching for a break in the traffic before attempting to cross the road. And she takes the opportunity to turn and start walking away again. I am not chasing after her. Whatever game she's playing can wait.

Shoulders back and boobs out, I turn toward the store. Here we go.

A bell jingles as I open the shop door and step into the air-conditioned space. There's a faint scent of lavender or something. Wooden racks hold rows of clothing sorted by color. Jewelry, shoes, hats, and some homewares are displayed on and around a long wooden table in the center of the store. There's even a display of vintage jackets and bags for sale. It all looks so good. I kind of want to buy everything.

A woman approaches me with a smile. She has dark skin, long hair, a cool floral tattoo on her arm, and is wearing one of the green linen jumpsuits displayed in the front window. There was a time in this town when women were cutting their hair short for safety's sake. All of the ones who went missing had long hair. The shop assistant's practiced eye takes in my old jeans, faded tank top, and the bedraggled sneakers on my feet. The fading bruise on my face has been carefully covered with concealer.

It's not like I've bought nothing in the last nine years. Once something wore out beyond repair, then I replaced it. But it was mostly just the basics, which I shopped for online. My therapist Heather would say I don't believe I deserve nice things. She'd say I have survivor's guilt.

The woman who works here stops and cocks her head. "Sidney?"

Her recognition is happening faster than I imagined. But if she asks me to leave, then okay. I'll just try somewhere else. This isn't the only clothing store in town.

"My name is Emma," she says. "I was a year below you in high school."

"Oh."

"Can I help with anything?"

"I need a couple of outfits. Maybe more than a couple."

"Okay," says Emma.

"This has started getting on my nerves." I wave my hand in the general direction of me. "I want to look better."

"I can help you with that."

A woman over by the changing rooms stops and stares at me. The hostility coming from her corner is a lot. But it's nothing

I haven't seen before. And at least she's not hissing murderer or whore at me. That shit really hurts my feelings.

Emma heads for the racks on the other side of the store. "How about I show you some things so I can gauge what you like and go from there?"

"That sounds great." I smile. "Don't suppose you know a good hairdresser?"

Kaia Kater is playing when we hear the front door open. Muriel and I are in the back of the house in the study, ready for our weekly meeting. Sunday brunch is the perfect time for blackberry scones. Though carbohydrates and sugar are always a solid idea.

Nothing was said about my new navy-and-white-stripe midi tank dress and light makeup. Same goes for the fresh long layers and strands of honey and platinum in my hair. Though I know she noticed, thanks to the definite widening of her eyes. Muriel's probably scared of saying anything in case I change my mind and run upstairs to scrub my face and put on a pair of sweatpants or something. And who can blame her?

Hana is running late, though that's not unusual. What is unusual is her remembering to use her key. Banging on the door and hollering is her preferred method of gaining entry to the house. But what's truly bizarre is how she's talking to someone. Same goes for the deep voice that answers.

Muriel raises her brows.

I know the voice, though I haven't heard it in three days. I wasn't sure if I'd ever hear it again. And now here he is, standing in my living room. Huh.

"…comes from this couple at the farmers' market they have just down the road," says Hana.

"Haven't gotten there yet," answers Noah.

"You have to go. So good."

"Nice pictures."

"Sidney's grandmother taught art," says Hana. "She did most of the prints and sketches. Nature was her favorite subject, as you can see."

He nods and looks around the room. This is not awkward at all.

I love my home. However, having him in it makes me doubt everything. The house has a simple layout. A living room at the front of the house with a fireplace on one side and stairs on the other. Then the kitchen, half bathroom, and a small, enclosed patio are on the right. While the dining room and study are on the left. Walls are a warm off-white with the original honey-colored wooden floorboards throughout. French doors with mottled glass separate the different rooms. Though I tend to leave them all open. Furniture is a mix of Grandma's and mine. Her midcentury teak dining table and my navy sofa. Her pair of vintage black leather and chrome armchairs and my blue velvet cushions and grey wool rug.

Our eyes meet, and yeah. I was so right about it being uncomfortable. His face is a careful blank. He just stands there in jeans and a tee with a black leather jacket and matching boots. I realize I've been so hungry for the sight and sound of him. I'm grateful to have him here. But this is not a helpful time to be ovulating.

Hana grins. "Doesn't Sidney look pretty?"

Noah just nods.

"Your neighbor was about to go for a ride. Did you know he had a motorcycle?"

I clear my throat. "No."

"Noah, this is Muriel. She's the third member of our group." Hana walks toward us, through the dining room and into the study. "This is what I wanted to show you."

I get to my feet with my mouth open, only I don't know what to say. Having someone new in my house is an odd enough occurrence. Showing him the contents of this room is on a whole other level.

Noah watches me in silence.

He doesn't seem like the sort of person who would tell the whole town what we're doing here. Secrecy around this project isn't do or die. However, I have no idea how the local police or anyone else would react to the news. Which makes me nervous. There are people still out there who believe I was behind the death and disappearances and that my ex is innocent. #justiceforryan is their cute catchphrase. They put it on tees and bumper stickers to help pay his legal fees and keep his name in the public eye.

I am the first to admit that the evidence can seem damning at first. One of my hairs was found on Briana Petersen's remains and a search of the area where her body was found had been performed on my computer. But cellphone data had me at home on the night she went missing. I was watching a film with my grandmother, who was able to provide me with an alibi. Ryan wound up being tied to the murder through his connection to me. There have been times when that has felt ironic as fuck. He had his cellphone turned off during the night in question and an eyewitness saw the victim with a man matching his description.

But back to the here and now. I'm curious what was said to get Noah over here. This could be Hana shooting my last shot. And realistically, the worst that can happen is he rejects me again. Like I don't have a bottle of tequila and a bag of limes ready to go. I shut my mouth and sit back down.

"There's a link between Sidney and Ryan's victims. Or the missing women who we believe were also his victims. They all had long hair and either attended or worked at or near the college," says Hana. "We know he took Sidney to the place where he buried the body of Briana Petersen. A couple of months later, heavy rain displaced the soil, and her remains became exposed. It was sheer luck that they found her."

His attention turns to the walls.

"Lot of places to hide dead bodies in Vermont," says Muriel in her usual dry tone.

Hana makes a noise of agreement. "We believe he also took Sidney to his other disposal sites. All of this is about figuring out where they are."

"He took you to a lot of places?" Noah asks me.

I nod. "We did a lot of hiking, and he would pick where we'd stop to rest."

"For years now, we've been trying to help Sidney remember all those spots," says Hana.

"That's what all of the pins in the map mean?" asks Noah.

"Yeah. We're pretty sure we've got them all."

Noah pauses and turns to me. "Did he ever hurt you?"

"No. I mean, not until the end." I shake my head. "But he could be controlling. I was young and stupid, and thought I was in love."

"The night they arrested him, he had a kill kit with him,"

says Muriel. "He brought a backpack into her apartment. It had duct tape, rope, and other things of that nature."

Noah blinks. "He was going to murder you?"

"Things hadn't been going so great." It isn't easy to meet his gaze. "I didn't like being told what to wear or how to behave. Not that he did that exactly. But I knew what the disappointed looks meant."

"A psychopath can come across as confident and charming. It's because they don't care about social norms," explains Hana. "They truly have no fucks to give and that can make them seem free and enlightened and above it all. But the manipulation and lack of empathy often becomes obvious to targets over time."

"They have trouble reading or mirroring emotions, even when it would benefit them," adds Muriel.

Noah raises his brows. "You've done a lot of research into this."

"Everyone needs a hobby," says Hana with a smile.

Muriel sits back in her chair. "This is about keeping that bastard in jail. But it's also about helping people. Thoughts and prayers don't do a damn thing. You wouldn't believe how many cold cases there are in this country. Let alone how many women go missing each year."

Hana nods soberly.

"So…Ryan's control over Sidney was slipping," continues Muriel. "And for him, we believe, it's all about control."

"He was really going to kill you," repeats Noah.

I raise my face. "Yes."

"How old were you?"

"Nineteen."

"You were just a kid." He stares at me for a moment. Then he gestures to the walls. "This is why you stay in town?"

"Yes."

He turns to Hana and says, "Thank you."

"No problem. Have a nice ride on your motorcycle!"

"Nice to meet you, ma'am," he says to Muriel. "Thank you for letting me intrude on your Sunday."

We all watch him leave. The heavy tread of his boots on the hardwood floor and the sound of the door closing shut behind him. He's the first person outside of our group to ever see this room and all the evidence of our almost decade-long obsession with death. And he didn't run screaming, which I am willing to take as a sort of win.

Muriel sighs. "I can't believe he ma'amed me. Though he does have excellent manners."

"Yeah. I really wasn't prepared for how much hotter he is up close," says Hana. "But I thought it went well. Don't you think it went well?"

"Jury's still out on that one. Did you tell Sidney you were bringing him in here?"

"I didn't even know I was going to do it," says Hana. "But then I saw him standing there and just thought…fuck it."

Muriel snorts.

Hana frowns in my direction. "Sidney, say something. I can take you salty, but I can't handle silence. Are you mad at me or what?"

"No."

"Are you sure?" she asks. "You look like you're experiencing big feelings."

"I am." I take a deep breath and let it out slowly. "But this is a good thing. He has all of the facts now and can make an informed decision as to whether he ever wants to talk to me again. Thank you."

Muriel's eyes widen for a second time today.

"You know, I refused to let Ryan control me. But that's exactly what I've been allowing the situation he caused do to me for years."

Hana nods sadly. "Yeah."

"Women often carry the shame for things they didn't do. The question is," says Muriel, "what are you going to do about it?"

I get to my feet and stand tall. "Who wants a margarita?"

CHAPTER FOUR

N O MATTER THE QUESTION, DAY DRINKING IS ALWAYS the answer. Our laughter and music meant I didn't hear the noises coming from outside until the late afternoon. No idea how long Noah's been in my backyard. No idea why he's in my backyard. Though the axe in his hands and pile of wood sitting neatly to the side offer some strong hints.

I grab him a beer out of the fridge. Hospitality was important to Grandma, and she trained me well. There's a hopeful smile on my face as I head on out and hand over the ice-cold bottle. It's got to be a positive sign—him being here performing manual labor.

"Just dealing with the tree limb that fell down during that storm," he says. He looks like lumberjack porn come to life, standing there all sturdy and strong in his jeans, boots, and a tee. So many muscles. Just all the muscles in all the land.

"I did call a handyman. Was just waiting for them to call me back and arrange a time."

He downs a mouthful of beer. "Now you don't need to worry about this. Just get them to replace the broken palings on the fence and your smashed mailbox."

"Okay. Thanks."

There's a fire pit made out of stone and a couple of Adirondack chairs. It's peaceful and private and all mine. A green space to sit and stare at the flames or look up at the stars. But not yet. The sky overhead is streaked with the colors of sunset. Orange and pink, violet and blue. I turn in a slow circle, taking it all in. It's like the world is putting on a show.

"How was your ride?" I ask.

"Good. Took Route 2 through the islands. It gave me time to think." He narrows his gaze on me. "Have you been drinking?"

"Yes."

"That explains the party I heard happening inside." He smothers a smile. "Did you have fun?"

"We really did."

"Good. Hana and Muriel gone now?"

I nod and sit my ass down before I fall down. Alcohol may or may not have been the actual best answer to my particular set of problems. But today was a heck of a lot of fun just the same. A dandelion grows in the grass beside my chair. Obviously, the universe wants me to make a wish. I blow on the dandelion and squeeze my eyelids shut tight.

"What'd you wish for?" he asks.

"If I tell you, it won't come true." I open my eyes and turn the dandelion around and around. "Grandma and I were always doing things like that when I was growing up. Wishing on shooting stars, eyelashes, tossing coins into fountains, and blowing out the candles on birthday cakes."

"Mm."

"Somewhere along the way, adulthood takes over and we lose our sense of wonder. One of the worst mistakes we ever make." Which is when something else occurs to me. "How did you even get out here?"

"The side gate was open."

Huh. Me and my stalker need to talk sooner rather than later. There's no way I left the gate unlocked. Standing across the street from me is one thing. But peeping in windows is right the fuck out. Which reminds me of something. I fetch my cell out of my left bra cup (the dress is great, but it has a distinct lack of pockets).

"Is it okay that I am here?" he asks.

"Yes."

"Makes sense that you'd be security conscious. I should have knocked and said something. I'll do that next time."

"Thank you."

And there's my stalker on the Justice for Ryan website under updates. Sometimes I really hate being right. But of course she's here following me around because of him. They met when she wrote to him about his tragic plight, apparently. It was love at first sight when she went to visit him. How lovely. The happy couple have high hopes of attracting the interest of a well-known organization that works to free people who've been wrongfully convicted. And I highly doubt it's going to happen with him being guilty as sin.

Interesting how he and I have both met new people this year. Though my ex is obviously doing better at love than I, despite being behind bars. Which both is and isn't funny. Whatever. There's no way I am wrecking what's been a great day by thinking about him and his loser girlfriend.

Soon summer will be over, and the maples will start to show their autumn colors. But for now, the birds are singing and bugs are chirping and everything is fine. Turns out a tequila buzz in the afternoon is a splendid thing. The sky overhead goes on forever, making me feel like anything is possible. Like I could start my life over and make fewer mistakes or different ones or something. It's a beautiful dream.

Grandma used to say if you're always bracing yourself for bad things, you miss the chance to enjoy good things. It can best be summed up as pessimism makes you a pissy person. No idea why I am remembering this now. But it feels relevant to my state of mind and how I've approached life for the last however many years.

"Have you been walking on your own at night?" he asks.

"No. I thought it'd be best to take a break from that."

He nods.

Having a stalker means being a bit more careful. Too many places for her to hide in the dark. But I am not getting into that with him. Not when I don't know where we stand.

"My marriage fell apart because we stopped making time to talk to each other," says Noah out of nowhere, taking the seat opposite me. "Both of us had stressful jobs and life was just so fucking busy. What did it matter if I didn't know exactly where she was at, and if she hadn't heard the latest bullshit from my work, you know?"

I listen.

"We wound up being nothing more than roommates." He stares off in the distance for a moment. "What I am trying to say is that open and honest communication is important to me."

"Okay."

"I get your point that we haven't known each other for long. And it's got to be hard for you to talk about these things."

"Yeah. Noah, I didn't know what he was doing. That he was hurting people."

"I know." And he seems so certain. So sure.

The relief running through me is immense. Though open and honest communication requires one more step. Thank goodness for fake courage care of the booze. "It's okay if you want to ask questions. We can talk about it."

"Are you sure?"

"Yes. It'd probably be good for me to practice getting it out there with someone new. Not having it be this thing always hanging over my head, you know?"

He pauses. "You'll tell me if you need to stop?"

I nod.

"What happened the night he was arrested? How far did he get with his plan to hurt you?"

I take my time, choosing my words with care. Thinking about this stuff sort of makes me want to vomit, but that's nothing new. And I'm sick of Ryan having this power over me. "He'd picked up pizza as an apology for a fight we had a few days before. Funnily enough it was about me cutting my hair. All of the women who had gone missing from campus had long hair and so most people were cutting theirs to be safe. The topic had come up a few times and he always made me feel like I was being stupid and wouldn't be as attractive with short hair. And that I should feel safe because didn't he always pick me up and walk me to and from classes when he could?"

Noah's lips are a flat unhappy line.

"He liked me worrying about the missing women. I think it made me more malleable. And of course, it made his secret self seem all the more terrifying and important," I say. "That night he was being so sweet, but I wasn't sure we were going to work out, which hurt because he was my first serious relationship. We were watching a movie. I can't remember what it was. Some of my memories of him are incomplete. My therapist says it's a trauma response."

"Is that why you've been having trouble tracking down the places he took you?"

"One of them," I say. "But we also did just go hiking that damn much. He liked to drive and of course he'd tampered with the tracking in his car so there are no records of exactly where we went. Muriel, Hana, and I have been checking weather maps, my class schedule, bank records, and anything else we can think of to try and fill in the gaps."

"Makes sense that he'd been trying to cover his tracks."

"He was organized. It's why it took them so long to catch him." A light breeze ruffles the leaves in the trees. I am safe, everything is fine, and my ex is locked up in a correctional facility. Which is exactly where he belongs. "That night there was no knocking or anything. No warning. The Tactical Services Unit broke down my apartment door. Scared the absolute crap out of me. But not Ryan. He immediately knew what was happening and went straight for me. The last thing he wanted to do before he got locked up was kill me."

"What did he do?"

"He tried to strangle me," I say. "We think that was his thing. His preferred method of homicide. Briana Petersen's body was very decayed and…you know…local wildlife. But the hyoid bone in her neck was broken. That's usually a pretty good indicator of strangulation."

"Right."

"He always tried to come across as this easygoing affable guy. The second the door broke his face changed. I don't know how to explain it. There was nothing of the person I thought I knew. It was like he'd never even existed. The whole good son and loving boyfriend had just been an act, you know?"

Noah nods.

"He grabbed my throat and squeezed as hard as he could. I remember the muscles in his arms popping…anyway. I couldn't talk for like a week and there were all these bruises." Some of my memories might be hazy; however, this one comes through loud and clear. The crushing pressure of his hands and the excitement shining in his eyes as darkness started creeping into my field of vision. Guess near-death experiences can be like that. Crystal clear and horrific and all kinds of fucked up.

"I am sorry that happened to you."

"Me too. It absolutely sucks that it happened. But I'm one of the lucky ones because I'm still alive."

He nods.

"I've decided it is time for me to get a life."

"How are you going to do that?"

"Good question." I lean my head back and stare at the sky. "I'm still working out the details. I think I'll start by making some lists and sort of go from there. Throw some possible ideas around and maybe make a plan, you know?"

His smile is amused.

"You doubt me, but I think this could work. The main problem as I see it is…I know who I used to be and what I used to enjoy. But I am not so sure anymore. Things have kind of stagnated for me over the last ten years. I kind of stagnated."

"Are you happy right now in this moment?"

I smile. "Yeah. I really am."

"Why don't you start from there?"

"Is it boring that I like hanging in my backyard, talking to you, and looking at the sky?"

"No."

"I do also enjoy some occasional day drinking and beating up my boxing bag."

"There you go," he says. "Balance in all things."

"You know, you're good at this."

"At what?"

"Making me feel good."

He downs a mouthful of beer and stares around the backyard. At the section of broken fence off to the side and his house beyond. "I think we should give being friends a try."

I do my best to ignore the sting. There's a silent *just* before the word *friends*. But at least he still wants to know me. "I'd like that."

We're not going on a date. This is two friends hanging out on a Monday night. Though it's still a great excuse to wear something new. Because at the end of the day, I dress for me and no one else. Your happiness can't rely on another person. It just doesn't work. This time my outfit is linen shorts and a matching camisole with flat sandals on my feet. The fit is sweet, though it makes me feel weirdly exposed. I don't usually go out in public with so much skin on display. I don't usually do anything to attract attention. But growth is my new best friend.

I am sitting on the front porch (another thing I don't tend to do) when Noah backs his vehicle out of the garage. He jumps out of his car to open the passenger-side door for me. Like a gentleman. He's wearing a pair of blue jeans, a white tee, and sneakers. The man does casual so well. His hair is wavy and brushed back from his face with a day or two worth of stubble on his jawline. I know we're just friends. But looking at him breaks my heart just a little. There's still this pull between us and it's going to take me a while to bury it deep.

I climb into the car. "Ever have to lock yourself out of your home because you keep wanting to change outfits?"

"No." He smiles. "But you look great."

"Thank you. So do you."

He closes my door and walks back around the front of the car to his side. His gaze takes in my fidgeting hands, and he asks, "You nervous?"

"I'm fine. Just the usual."

"You still want to do this, though, right?"

"Yes."

"Good. Thought we could go to the drive-in," he says, backing the car out onto the road. "That way we're out, but still have our own space."

"That's a great idea. I haven't been since I was a kid."

Music plays and a warm wind is blowing through the car windows as we drive north. The vibe in the vehicle is relaxed. I give him a basic rundown about my data entry job (the key point again being that it's boring but pays the bills). And he tells me about farms he's found in the local area whose wares he's eager to try. His knowledge of foodstuffs is awe inspiring.

There's no longer any need to worry about what he does or doesn't know about me. And since it's clearly established that we're friends, any overt sexual tension seems diffused by the time we reach our destination. It's nice that we can just relax and enjoy ourselves. I'm happy the night is delivering on the reasons Noah moved to New England. Maybe it means he'll stay.

The sun is setting as the first film starts. It's a family-friendly animated movie about animals running wild in a city. Noah hits the snack bar and returns with dinner.

"Most mediocre nachos I've ever tasted," he says, wiping his hands with a napkin.

"Yeah. But the cheeseburgers make up for it."

"They are excellent."

"If you could only eat one thing for the rest of your life, which would you choose," I ask, "onion rings or mozzarella sticks?"

"Those are the only two options?"

"Yes."

"I'm going to have to go with the sticks. What about you?"

"Same," I say. "Onion rings are great. But the answer is always cheese."

"Very true. What about between corn dogs and hot dogs?"

"That's a tough call. I'm honestly not sure. Do I want the crunch of the corn or the softness of the bread? Both can come with a stupid amount of ketchup, so that doesn't help. Which do you choose?"

He pops another fry in his mouth. "It's truly a question for the ages. How about apple pie logs and fried Oreos?"

"I feel like I should say apple pie logs because fruit."

"But deep down you really want the Oreo."

"I really do. Chocolate is just so great." I take a sip from my bottle of water. "Is there anything the human race hasn't tried to deep fry?"

"I don't think so."

"It's what separates us from the animals."

"Yeah," he agrees. "That kid's enjoying himself."

I look over my shoulder to see the small child in the car next to us blowing raspberries on the window. The tongue waggling really adds something. Not something good. Just something.

"Do you want children?" I ask.

"That's not a first date question."

"This isn't a date."

His smile is there and gone in an instant. Guess you could call it rueful. "I don't know. Maybe. With the right person. What about you?"

"Same."

"They seem like a hell of a lot of work. Not something you just want to rush into."

"No," I say. "It's a big decision. Being responsible for bringing a whole new person into the world."

We both watch the film for a while. There's a small chance I shouldn't have asked such a personal question. I'm not exactly up to date with etiquette. But with him knowing the worst thing about me, it seems any boundaries are unsubstantial at best. And he did talk to me about his divorce. So, he must trust me at least a little.

The first film ends. Coming in second is an action and adventure movie. A car chase followed by a gunfight with the discovery of a lost city thrown in for good measure. I think it's fun, though the couple sitting inside the flatbed truck in front of us get distracted. Noah and I might not be on a date, but they obviously are. And we've got a prime view of all their activities care of a back window.

It starts with the dude sliding his arm around her shoulders. Running his fingers through her hair and such. The way he touches her is adoring. Like she's precious to him. And the answering tug low in my belly when he pulls on her ponytail is interesting to say the least. I lost my libido a long time ago. When the only person you allowed near your vagina for sexual purposes turns out to be a murderous monster…yeah. It's hard to come back from something like that. My therapist has given me many a lecture on the topic.

The couple progresses to kissing. More tongue than necessary to my mind. Though I'm probably not the best judge. I doubt my mouth even remembers how to get the job done. And by the time Ryan got arrested, he had started getting heavy handed with me. Not hitting me. Just being way too full on. Trying to take over every moment. Being physically rough with me. Another sign of him trying to control me.

One day I will find someone and do a whole lot of sexing. So much that all of the bad memories of sleeping with my ex will fade into nothing. They'll be no more than a bad dream. Though the sexing probably won't happen around here. I never wanted to hear how someone had hooked up with me for the novelty. That they banged me so they could have a connection to a psychopath or something. Have a sordid story to tell over drinks with friends. I might be overly sensitive. But on the other hand, people do all sorts of strange and distasteful shit for fun.

In the meantime, I might as well enjoy the show. Not the one on the screen. The one where the girl is now sitting in the guy's lap. Her hands are in his hair and his are busy out of sight. On her breasts maybe. I check over my shoulder. Luckily the small mouthy child has fallen asleep. Sex is all good and natural and normal. But his parents may not be ready to tackle the subject just yet nor in this particular setting.

I take another sip of water. "Do you think they have an exhibition kink?"

"I was just wondering that. Though sometimes I guess you just can't wait until you get home."

"Mm."

"Their windows are starting to steam up." Noah tosses some popcorn into his mouth. "You know you're getting old when you see something like this and think a bed would be so much more comfortable."

"It would, though. You're just being practical."

"Thanks," he says with a smile.

"I didn't know people still did this at the drive-in."

"Pretty sure they're not supposed to do this in public."

"Imagine telling your child they were conceived at the movies."

"I was conceived somewhere over Nebraska while my parents were busy joining the Mile High Club."

My mouth falls open like it's come unhinged. "No. Really?"

He nods.

"Is it wrong that I love how your parents told you that?"

"Sort of." He grins. "What about you?"

"Not a clue. My mom died when I was little, and my dad was never in the picture."

"I'm sorry."

"Thanks. But I was lucky. I had my grandma, and she was amazing."

"Did you have any other family around?" he asks.

"A cousin who used to stay in the summers. We were really

close there for a while. But Grandma was kind of a free spirit and not to everyone's tastes. My aunt and her didn't really get along, so we were usually just our own little family unit."

"Nice."

There's now some definite up-and-down movements happening in the flatbed truck. We both watch in silence for a moment. As you do. But a woman with a flashlight is coming this way, walking down the aisle between cars. She bypasses us and knocks on the window of the truck.

"Oops," I say.

"Busted," agrees Noah.

The lovers separate as the woman with the flashlight does some finger-wagging at them. Threats are made. It's all very dramatic and we're not the only ones watching them instead of the screen. Though their conversation is carried out in low voices in due deference to the film. Which is highly unhelpful.

"What do you think they're saying?" asks Noah.

"Well…the dude is all sheepish. He knows they're cooked. But his girl is going full-on denial. Look at her shaking her head and staring down her nose at the woman. She is shocked and stunned by these baseless accusations. How dare her reputation be besmirched in such a fashion."

"That's what she's saying?"

"Yeah."

"She actually used the word *besmirched*?"

"She did. Big feelings deserve big words. Though *besmirched* is only two syllables, so…" I smile. "Our valiant hero, the lady from the snack bar, is having none of this bullshit, however. She knows exactly what sort of shenanigans have been going on and is banning both of them."

"Can't really blame her."

"No. But girlfriend doesn't know when to stop. Because she's opening her mouth to keep arguing. And if that doesn't work, she might even think about weaponizing her tears. Which is when snack bar lady says…'don't make me summon a higher authority.'"

Noah raises an eyebrow. "Do you mean her manager or God?"

"I was actually referring to the police. Indecent exposure, disorderly conduct…"

"Gotcha."

"Though I'd be damn impressed if she managed to summon God."

"That would be something," he agrees.

Sure enough, the conversation winds down as the scolded couple climb back into their vehicle. This time, sitting a short distance apart. And just in time, since the small child in the car beside us has awoken and is back to licking the window.

"Thanks for doing this with me tonight," I say.

"Anytime. I mean it, Sid."

The couple in front of us start to kiss. Again.

"You're kidding me," drawls Noah.

"They sure are determined. Humanity is wild." I steal a handful of popcorn from the box he's holding. Then I probably go too far by saying, "Imagine if this had been our first date. That could have been us getting busted."

But he just laughs. I think it's my favorite sound in the whole wide world.

CHAPTER FIVE

TUESDAY IS GROCERY SHOPPING DAY. SOMETHING I enjoy more than I probably should. It's all of the choices in the cookie aisle. They excite me. But also, Hana is right. People need to get used to me. With this in mind, I don't wear baggy clothing and a ball cap to hide amongst the masses. The navy-and-white-stripe tank midi dress with a pair of flat sandals is fine for running errands. I even went for a walk to the lake during daylight hours.

The thing is, it's been years since I've been in the news or the main topic of discussion in this town. What are the odds most have moved on and no longer recognize me or care about me? It's hit or miss, I think, as a woman in a hot-pink pantsuit recognizes me and gives me a reassuring smile in the cheese section. Which is nice.

Being watched isn't anything new. And I was raised to believe women should take up space. That we can be loud and bright and whatever the hell we want. Grandma would be appalled if she'd known I'd strayed from this belief.

I am way overthinking the purchase of some apples when I feel a fresh set of eyes on me. Up close this time. Just on the other side of the display. And there stands my stalker. Her long blonde hair hangs like a silk curtain around her face. I'd honestly kill to know her hair care routine.

"I was wondering when I'd see you again," I say. "What do you think, Honeycrisp or Gala? Do you have a preference?"

"Ryan says hello." Her voice is pitched just perfectly, sweet and vaguely evil. This is all so extra. She hasn't done anything to hurt me. Not yet anyway. It might not be smart to screw with her, but I'm so sick of being scared. Though if she pulls a gun out of her bag, she could definitely have the last laugh. "He didn't want you to think he'd forgotten about you, Sidney."

"That's the message you were sent to deliver, huh?" I ask. "Laura, girl to girl, have you tried touching grass?"

The smile disappears.

"What do you get out of dating him? Or to use therapy speak, what need does being with him fulfill in you?" I cock my head. "I mean, I get that you know where he is and what he's doing all the time and there's a sense of safety in that. You're totally in control. It's not like he can cheat on you and there's no chance of him hanging around messing up your house or getting physical with you either. And between you and me, that last one is kind of a biggie when it comes to him."

Nothing from her.

"Or is it the infamy of being known as his better half? Are you hoping for some time in the spotlight? A little of that local fame?"

She just glares at me.

"You don't strike me as having a savior complex.

Thinking you'll be the one to deliver him from this supposed injustice. But I've been wrong before. Or maybe you accept that he's a murderous motherfucker and think your sweet love can change him. Stop him from being a monster and put him on the right path."

"You don't know a fucking thing."

"I know that you can't teach empathy," I say. "You can't make him care about other people. He just mimics emotions, turns on the charm, and uses coercive control to get what he wants."

Her gaze is hard and sharp. The girl doesn't appreciate the truth bombs. "He said you'd be too scared to call the cops on me."

"It's a complicated situation. But I would really appreciate it if you stayed off my property in the future."

Due to her use of an outside voice and swearing, we're attracting attention. A man with a baby gives us definite side eye. And a young person standing over by the bananas pulls out their cell to film the confrontation. Which is when Laura decides to take her leave. It's not the sort of attention she's after, apparently. Though the security cameras didn't bother her. I don't know. She's a strange one.

I straighten my shoulders and push my shopping cart in the opposite direction. Everything is fine. Just ignore how my hands are shaking. Seems I may not be completely cool with getting stalked by this bitch after all. But I have things to look forward to—like bingo tonight with Muriel and beating the shit out of my punching bag when I get home. A mostly healthy release for a messed-up situation. "Sweater Weather" by The Neighbourhood starts playing over the speaker system and yes. I love this song. Some lucky people in the bakery section even get to hear me singing it. Grocery store soundtracks really can save the day.

Hana texts me during breakfast on Wednesday.

Hana: How did your date go?

Me: Not a date. Just friends.

Hana: Answer the question.

Me: Good. He's having drinks with work friends at his house on Sunday.

Hana: He asked you to go?

Me: Yeah.

Hana: Will you?

Me: I think so.

Hana: Do it do it do it.

Me: Bingo was fun. I had no idea it was so competitive. A fight nearly broke out. And I'm pretty sure another couple are getting a divorce.

Hana: Invite me next time. I need to experience this.

Me: Will do. Wanna catch a movie next week?

Hana: I would love to!

Hana: But I have some bad news.

Me: What?

Hana: I really don't want to tell you. But you
need to know. Sorry.

She sends me a link. It's the first trailer for a series coming soon to a streaming service. Creepy music plays. Two men are seated at a table surrounded by the microphones and computers required for a podcast. They talk about the fear felt by the citizens of this city when the hunt was on for a killer.

Photos flash up on screen of Ryan and me together. Me sitting on his lap at a concert in a park. Us posing happily with a bunch of flowers he bought me for Valentine's Day. These are followed by video of me testifying in court and a picture of Briana Petersen. Then we're following a winding path through the woods leading to a realistic-looking skull lying on the ground. It's all very gross and dramatic.

Next, Ryan is heard speaking over the phone from jail. My stomach turns upside down at the sound of his voice. It's been so long since I heard it. He swears I manipulated him into taking part in the murder and helping me dispose of the body out in the woods. The poor innocent man is just a victim of love, apparently. Which is not a new thing. To clear him or knock down the charges in the original court case meant his legal team needed to prove reasonable doubt. Apparently, the easiest way of doing so was by shifting the blame to someone else. Me. The strand of my hair on Briana Petersen's body and the search of her burial site on my computer created enough doubt that the jury would only convict him of manslaughter.

I assume the documentary makers are just ignoring the other women who went missing during the time he spent at school. No need to unduly complicate the tale of his supposed innocence.

He claims therapy has helped him to understand how I coerced and controlled him. How pressure from me led to him playing a part in this terrible tragedy. I was jealous of Briana Petersen, apparently. Which is news to me. But he says he's spent the time in jail praying for forgiveness. He credits finding religion and his real love with turning his life around. Which is when my stalker, Laura, gets her share of the limelight. How nice.

I had assumed she was attracted to him because he was a psychopath. However, maybe I am wrong about that. She might just be with him because she believes he was done wrong by society and the justice system. You never know. Though her behavior tends to lean toward idolizing and mimicking homicidal assholes more than anything. What I've seen of it, at least.

The scene returns to the podcasters, who promise new interviews with officials involved in the investigation. Along with family and friends of both the accused and the victim. It finishes with the announcement that they will be shedding new light on the case. They're calling it *Misled* and over fifty thousand people have watched the trailer already.

Bile rushes up the back of my throat. I make it to the bathroom just in time to vomit up breakfast.

Sometimes a girl just needs to rot in bed. To turn her back on the world and wither for a while. Which is exactly what I am in the process of doing when my neighbor starts shouting at eleven o'clock at night. So rude.

"I know you're there and I know you're awake, so come to the window." Noah pauses. "Come on, Sid."

The problem with his request is twofold. One. I don't want to. And two. Just more of the same, actually. For him to be yelling at my window like this means he has seen the trailer. Awkward as fuck. Just horrendous.

"Will you come to the window, please?" he pleads again.

I remember what the other problem is now. I look like shit. My eyes are puffy and red from crying. And while I didn't used to mind so much about my appearance, apparently my care factor on this front has shifted. Especially when it comes to my neighbor with whom I am just good friends.

"For me?"

Dammit. He found my weakness. I haul my sorry self off the bed and stretch the various kinks out of my back. It was daylight when I laid down, but now it's dark as...well...night.

"I have ice cream," he yells across the divide.

"You should've said that to start with," I say. "What kind?"

"Belgian chocolate and, ah, maple butter pecan."

"Give me the maple butter pecan," I say, heading for the window. "Hi."

He gives me a small smile and wraps the pint in a towel. Next, he winds some thick string around the whole thing and ties it off with a bow. "Ready?"

I nod, and he carefully tosses the parcel between our two houses. It's a quiet night. With the exception of all the noise we're making. He even thought to include a spoon. Talk about a full-service bedroom-to-bedroom ice cream delivery system. I rest my butt on the windowsill, and we eat in silence for a minute or two. Each of us with our respective pints. Sugar always helps. It's just science.

"Your place is locked up tight, right?" he asks. "You're safe?"

"Yes."

"Good. And I know that you can look after yourself, but I worry."

I don't know what to say. Though his words loosen something inside of me. Like suddenly it's easier to breathe and exist.

"Someone sent back the bacon and clam chowder tonight because there was bacon in it," he says.

"You'd think the name would give it away."

"You would."

"It's like me being mad because there's pecan in this ice cream. What do you do when that sort of thing happens?" I ask, digging my spoon in deep.

"Just comp them something else. It isn't worth the hassle of causing a scene or getting a bad review. Everyone makes mistakes now and then."

I nod. "That's a very adult way of looking at it."

Noah is dressed in his work uniform. Black pants and a white tee. The bedroom light shines behind him. Seeing the lines of his face and hearing the depth of his voice does make life better. It's strange how people have different vibes. Way back when, I would get excited to see my ex. But being with him didn't soothe me in this way.

He watches me for a minute and then asks, "Do you want to talk about the trailer?"

Good question. The answer is both yes and no. Ugh. "There've been podcasts about what happened. But never an actual show before. I wonder if someone will write a book."

"Did you get asked to go on any of the podcasts?"

"Yeah. And there have been interview requests from

newspapers and magazines. Talk shows who wanted me to come on and trauma dump. I always say no."

"You never wanted to tell your side of the story?"

"That's the thing…there was so much said about me even from the start. Most of it complete bullshit from people I'd never met. The idea that anything I could say would affect that barrage one way or another always seemed so farfetched."

He nods.

"These people turn me into content. They reduce my life and these horrible fucked-up experiences down to soundbites and clickbait. I don't know how I'm supposed to feel about that," I say with no small amount of anger. "Do you think I should talk to them?"

"No. Not if you don't want to. Fuck 'em. None of them actually care about you. At the end of the day, most of them are just trying to profit off your pain."

I think it through for the thousandth time. And he's right.

"I take it they don't need your permission then to use photos or video of you or whatever?"

"No. It's all a matter of public record now."

This makes him scowl.

I like having Noah on my side. Both him and ice cream are top-tier things. He licks the chocolate ice cream off his spoon and whoa. What a hussy. I really need to start being a better friend and stop sexualizing this man.

"Can I ask you something personal?"

He nods.

"How did you know that you wanted to get married? That they were the one you thought you should be with for the rest of your life?"

This elicits a sigh from him. "We'd been together a few years when she asked me."

"She asked you?"

"Yeah." He smiles. "Beatriz knew what she wanted. I always liked that about her. She was going to make manager where she worked and put a down payment on an apartment and all sorts of things. She was going places, and I loved her, so I wanted to go with her."

I wait.

"We were both working long hours and giving our jobs everything. Making head chef at a great restaurant was what I'd always wanted. But I came home one night and realized I hadn't seen her in almost a week. We would text each other about paying bills and feeding the cat and not a hell of a lot else. That's not much of a marriage. Things had been falling apart for so long we didn't even know where to start trying to put it back together."

"That must have hurt you both."

"It wasn't acrimonious as these things go, and it's been a year now." He shrugs. "Sitting here eating ice cream with you isn't so bad. I kind of feel like I've landed on my feet."

I raise my pint in toast to the man.

"People have this idea of love like if it's real it'll all just be okay. But that's not how things go. You have to want it enough to put in the work," he says. "Anyway…I'm in no rush to get serious with someone again. Dating casually is one thing. But going through a divorce was a lot."

"Time to relax and enjoy your life."

"That's right," he says with a nod. "Enough of my shit. Give me a rundown of your romantic history."

"That won't take long." I smile. Then I stop smiling. "I

thought I loved Ryan and that he was the one. But I didn't even really know him…just who he was pretending to be. The mask he wore to blend in with the general public and pretend to be normal."

"Has there been anyone since?"

"No."

He watches me in silence.

"Today was trash," I say. "But tomorrow will be better."

"Not tonight?"

"No." I shake my head. "Tonight is for wallowing and feeling shitty."

He puts down his pint and pulls his cell out of his pants pocket. A few taps on the screen later, music starts playing. "You need the right ambience for that."

"What is this?" I ask. "Adele?"

"Yeah."

"Noah, you can't just play something like this without warning people. It's so sad. You can actually hear her heart breaking."

"So fucking sad," he agrees. "I play it in my car when I feel like crying."

I laugh softly.

"You mock my pain."

"Sorry. My bad."

"How about this one," he says, tapping another button on his screen. "The Night We Met" by Lord Huron plays next.

"Oof. This is a doozy."

"I know, right?"

"It's like musically having your heart gouged out with a fork."

"That's disturbingly graphic, but apt. I also occasionally

like to stare into the abyss and despair of life to this one." He plays another song. The version of "Hallelujah" by Jeff Buckley.

"Having an existential crisis to this song is honestly an appropriate response."

"Glad you approve."

I stab my spoon into the softened ice cream. Seems you can in fact eat too much sugar. "You've completely derailed my wallowing. Shame on you."

"I'd hope you're still feeling at least a little shitty. You seemed so set on tonight being the worst. I would hate to trash that for you."

"Nope. You've completely wrecked my plans," I say. "Thanks."

He stares at me for a moment and smiles, and I have to remind myself again—just friends. He doesn't want anything romantic and I can and will respect that. But each moment I spend with him, my heart seems to slip a little farther out of my reach.

CHAPTER SIX

"**A**N ICED COFFEE WITH SKIM MILK AND A SHOT OF butterscotch syrup, please," I say with a smile bordering on rigor mortis. My face is aching from holding this sucker in place. It's Thursday morning and I have decided to come at the world with the energy I hope to see. Therefore, I am being the politest, most boundary-respecting bitch in all of time and space.

Wide eyes blink at me from behind the counter. "You're that girl."

"Yes."

The barista mumbles something and gets busy with my order. No idea what he said. I don't really want to know. Any hope people had been starting to forget about my existence has been obliterated, and there's nothing I can do about it. The trailer is sitting pretty at a quarter of a million views. And you just know ninety percent of those views are probably from the citizens of this fair city. Briana Petersen and my ex and I are back in the news. However, I am not going back into hiding.

There's a sort of alert stillness to the people behind me in line. Like when someone is busy listening into your conversation.

You can feel their focus on you. "They're filming down at the lake," says the lady over my shoulder.

"What did you say?" I ask with my smile still in place.

"For the documentary."

"Oh." My stomach sinks. This is some unfortunate fucking news on a bright sunny day. I thought they made trailers after they'd finished making a show. Guess not always. I turn back to the barista. "Make it two shots of syrup, please."

"I saw them down there with a camera crew." Her tone isn't judgmental or anything. Just your usual level of interest in something salacious. She's wearing a shirt with a picture of a cat on it, and I respect her fashion choice.

A young man stands waiting behind her wearing a Red Sox cap. "A bunch of them are staying at the Hilton."

"They were in earlier with big orders," says the barista. "Made the boss real happy."

"The local economy could certainly do with the boost. But I don't believe his story one bit," the woman confides in me. She might not, but the dude behind her is squinting down his nose at me. Like I might pull a weapon at any moment.

"Can I have whipped cream too, thanks?" I ask the barista. Because eating and drinking your feelings are valid. And the skim milk balances out the sugar and cream when you think about it. I hold my card to the machine to pay for the order and then move aside.

"It'll be interesting to see what the new evidence is," says the young man in a tone suggesting his words hold much weight. Such an open-minded and unbiased point of view. We are blessed to be in the presence of one of the great minds of our age.

My hero, Cat Shirt Lady, is having none of it, however. "A court of law already found him guilty."

"Yeah, but they might not have had all the information." His suspicious gaze slides to me.

Give me strength. I can now vividly recall why I went into hiding in the first place. Why I decided it was better to be silent and anonymous. Situations such as this. Strangers in the street speculating about my guilt or innocence. Though the first time around I was a teenager overwhelmed and out of my depth. Now I am a salty almost thirty-year-old who has had enough. In other words, there comes a time when being polite no longer serves you.

I pick up my drink, turn to the young man, and say, "You're being a dick."

His eyebrows reach for the sky.

"I am a real person standing right here just trying to live my life and purchase caffeine."

Guess he didn't expect me to defend myself. The poor man is aghast. "I am entitled to my opinion!"

"Yes. You absolutely are. But it takes a special kind of asshole to shove that opinion unasked for in my face."

"Don't think you're supposed to swear at other customers," says the barista helpfully.

I take a sip of my drink. "This is really good. Thank you."

"You're welcome."

The young man is now in a high state of agitation. "That's all you're going to say to her?"

The barista shrugs. "I gave her a warning."

"You did," I agree. "I am so warned. Thanks again."

"Have a nice day."

"But…" splutters the young man.

Meanwhile, Cat Shirt Lady is standing at the counter ready to give her order. "Oh, shove a sock in it, would you?"

I open the door and step into the sunshine. While this encounter could have gone better, it could also have gone a heck of a lot worse. And I would be lying if I said there wasn't a small but authentic smile on my face as I walked home.

The knock on my door comes around sunset. Noah is at work, Hana is on a date, Muriel is out of town, and Mateo left like an hour ago. All of the people I'm willing to open the door for at this hour are accounted for. I put down my water bottle on the kitchen counter and pick up my cell. And the person the camera shows standing outside is a major surprise.

I rush to open the door. "Grace?"

"Hey." My cousin's smile is cautious. "It's been a minute."

"Yeah. What are you doing here?"

Her smile wavers.

"I mean, you're welcome of course. It's great to see you."

"But it's been a minute," she repeats with her grin back in place.

"It really has." I step back. "Come on in."

Grandma had two daughters—my mother and Grace's. Aunt Beth moved away for college and did her best to never come back. She works for a bank in Manhattan. But every summer when we were children, Grace was sent to stay in Vermont. We'd go swimming at the lake and do all sorts of things together. This lasted until we were fourteen or so, when she wanted to stay in the city with friends. We texted and stayed in touch for a while. But we haven't really been in contact for the last nine years or so.

When we were children, I used to pretend that we were sisters. Because we used to look sort of similar, with the same dark blonde hair. Though now hers has been dyed a rich mahogany. And my hair is shoulder length, while hers reaches halfway down her back. She's wearing a beige slip dress with fine gold necklaces and white sneakers. While I'm back to wearing my old blue jeans and a tank. Though to be fair I had planned on cleaning, and was not expecting company.

She steps up to give me a hug. One of those where their body is rigid and kept at a careful distance from yours. It makes sense we aren't immediately comfortable with each other after all this time. And not everyone is a natural-born hugger. I choose not to take this as a bad omen.

A shiny new luxury hatchback is parked outside. The shadows are lengthening as the last light from the sun streaks the sky. I lock the door and face her with a smile both polite and puzzled.

"Long story short," she says. "Turns out my fiancé was cheating on me."

"No. What a bastard."

"He kicked me out of our apartment and caused trouble for me at work. I thought getting out of the city for a while would be helpful. Give all the drama a chance to die down."

"That's awful. I didn't even know you were engaged."

"Yeah. You can see why the idea of being somewhere different appealed. Give myself a chance to get my shit together and figure out what life is going to look like now. I would have called to warn you I was on my way, but I don't have your new number. You and I always had such good times here during the summers. Guess I was feeling nostalgic." She smiles. "Remember how Grandma would play classical music at top volume? She was always saying it was the original pop and punk music, and we should know where things came from."

"I remember those lectures well."

"And how she used to pay us to pull weeds?" she asks. "I swear I still have calluses on both my knees."

"We needed money for ice cream and movies. Though I distinctly remember you sunbathing around the corner of the house where Grandma couldn't see while I did the gardening for both of us."

"That doesn't sound like me at all." Grace laughs. Then she gives me this sad sort of smile. "Remember when we were little and we used to spend hours searching for four-leaf clovers?"

"That was a long time ago."

"I am sorry I disappeared on you. Would you believe I didn't know what to say? And then Gran died, and Mom was so angry about you getting the house. She made it this whole big thing. God…the way she would go on about it. It was like she was obsessed or something."

"Yeah. Her feelings were pretty clear at the funeral."

"But we're family, and I should have tried harder."

Guess it's my turn to not know what to say. This is the thing when someone comes back. Whatever faith you used to have in the person is gone. Showing her how much she hurt me by not reaching out during my worst days isn't an option. Because being vulnerable requires a level of trust we don't have right now. Though she did make the trip up here and I could definitely use more friends.

"I saw the trailer for the documentary," she says with a

wince. "How are you doing with all of that?" Before I can answer she's off and talking again. "I mean, having people know your name and being sort of famous must be at least a little fun, right?"

"It's not the kind of situation where people give you free coffee or other perks. And the stares are more along the lines of 'is she going to pull an axe out of her handbag and kill us all' as opposed to 'wow, check her out, she's so cool.'"

Her enthusiasm dims. "Well, what do you think of the documentary?"

"Eh. The less said the better. Let's talk about something else."

"Fair enough." Her smile disappears for a moment before returning to full force. "Do you still like to lie out in the backyard and howl at the moon?"

"It's been a while since I did that. But I mean, someone has to, right?"

"Yeah." She sighs. "You know I wasn't even sure where I was heading at first. Just got in the car and started driving north. It would be great if we could spend some time together. I booked a room at a cheap hotel out by the highway. You wouldn't believe how broke my ass is. All the money had been going toward paying for the big day. I spent like an hour on the phone to the baker yesterday arguing about a two-thousand-dollar deposit on a cake."

"Ouch. That's a lot of cake." My mouth opens and closes. Like the words don't want to come out. "Stay here. I have a spare room. Though it's a little messy. Storage boxes and things."

Her smile widens with relief. "Really?"

"Yeah. Of course," I say, convincing us both. "Like you said, we're family."

Bright sunlight borders the curtains by the time I wake the next morning. It took forever to get to sleep. My brain wouldn't shut up and shut down. And hearing my cousin moving around didn't help. She went downstairs for a glass of water or something multiple times. In the end, I got up and worked for a while. It's one of the benefits of data entry. You generally get to set your own work hours.

When I finally did get to sleep in the small hours of the morning, I had one of my favorite recurring nightmares. The one where I know my ex is somewhere close by. He's hunting me as I stumble down hallways and through darkened rooms. Looking for a way out or something I can use as a weapon. But there's nothing that might help me and every window and door is locked tight. His brutally strong hands grab at my neck and… this is where I wake up covered in sweat, gasping for breath.

Trauma sucks.

I realize that it was the sound of people talking that woke me. Not coming from inside the house, but from below my open window at the ruined section of the fence. Noah's voice I recognize straight away. However, it takes me a minute to remember that my cousin is currently a guest, and the other voice is hers. My brain isn't great first thing. Or the first few hours. And I am not used to sharing my space. Hana has crashed here a time or two after we stayed up late talking or binge watching something. Though I think she's probably the only one. Which reminds me. I grab my phone and text Hana, who responds immediately.

Me: How did your date go?

Hana: You know how the parmesan comes in
a shaker?

Me: Yeah.

Hana: He ate the whole thing.

Me: All the parmesan?

Hana: Yes.

Me: How full was it?

Hana: Full.

Me: That's amazing.

Hana: Definitely not lactose intolerant.

Me: Cheese monster.

Hana: Cheese maniac.

Me: Did he let you have any?

Hana: I would have hurt him otherwise.

Me: Fair enough.

Me: You going to see him again?

Hana: Yes. He's cute and I need to know what
other wild shit he does. This is now my purpose
in life.

Me: HA.

I push my hair out of my face. Stretch and yawn. The conversation continues below my window. And it's not like I am

trying to creep on them and listen, but it's rude to interrupt. Best to keep quietly listening and wait for a break like a civilized person. Noah stands with a hammer in his hand and new fence palings lay at his feet. Grace, meanwhile, is smiling and laughing and touching his arm. There's a chance it's the angle I am looking from, though she seems to be standing quite close to my neighbor, who is just a friend. Seriously close to him. Weirdly so. Inappropriately so.

There's finally a pause in their conversation, so I lean out the window and say, "Hello."

Grace turns her megawatt smile my way. Guess she's a morning person. I'd heard they existed, but never quite believed.

Noah tips his chin at me. "Figured I'd take a look at the fence."

"I did call another handyperson. They were going to drop by later this week."

"Now you can tell them they don't need to. Your cousin let me around back. Hope that's okay."

"Of course."

Grace laughs. "You look like you need coffee, girl."

"Yeah. I do."

I am not jealous. It would just be easier to face the world if the two of them didn't look so good together. Noah is, as usual, a visual delight in a pair of jeans and a tee with a backwards ball cap on his head. While Grace has blown-out hair, full makeup, and is wearing a pair of linen shorts with a cream knit tank. Her fit is fire. The way her long hair tumbles down her back in perfect curls. How many hours has she been awake for? And why is she yet again touching my Noah?

I mean neighbor. My neighbor. *Shit.*

Grace is back inside by the time I head downstairs after see-ing to the essentials. Which includes applying concealer, mas-cara, and a lip stain. Today I'm wearing a black maxi sundress with shoestring straps. Not only does it have pockets, but it feels dramatic. I had forgotten how dressing could be fun when you're not always trying to hide.

"How do you have it?" asks Grace, pouring coffee into a pair of mugs.

"Creamer and one sugar. Thanks."

"I wasn't sure how late you like to sleep, so I made myself at home."

And this is absolutely a good thing. Though I locked the door to the research room last night before going to bed. I'm happy to see Grace. But explaining the contents of that room requires a long and involved conversation. One I need to work myself up to having with people.

"Heartbreak and humiliation seem to be messing with my sleep routine, so…"

"That sucks," I say with a frown.

"Yeah. There's a plate of pancakes in the fridge. You used to love those, right?"

"I still do."

"Made them with Grandma's secret recipe."

"Pancake mix fresh out of the box?"

She gives me a wink. "When only the best will do. I trust you have some good real maple syrup to go with them?"

"Like they let you live in the state without it. I should ask Noah if he wants some."

"I already did," she says, "he said maybe later."

We settle in the dining room next door. It's impossible to

be upset when you have pancakes. They just make the world a better place to be. In fact, her flirting with my neighbor doesn't even matter. She peruses the accumulated junk on my table with an interested eye. A solid half of the space has been left clear for use. The rest has been given over to the detritus of my day-to-day life. Brochures, bills, and books mostly. Grace picks up a paperback. Not the one about starting a vegetable garden in your backyard. Nope. Not the monster fucking romance either. A shame, because they would have made for lighter conversation.

"*Mindhunter*," she reads from the cover. "Is this about those serial killer profilers at the FBI?"

"Yeah."

"I watched some of the TV series. Do you read much true crime?"

"It's sort of part of a research-project-type thing. Guess I kind of have a love-hate relationship with the genre."

"Makes sense."

"Do you think?"

"Yes." She takes a sip of coffee. "If it were me, I would want to understand what happened. Not only why he did the horrible things he did, but how other people in similar situations handled it."

"Hmm. I keep thinking I'll find something that explains everything. Just lays it all out for me. But I never do. My therapist thinks reading this stuff is bordering on being an unhealthy obsession."

"What would they know?"

I snort. "Supposed professionals, right?"

"How often do you do therapy?"

"Once a month if my brain is being nice to me."

She gives me a half smile. "In other news, your neighbor is hot as fuck."

"We're just friends."

"I was actually thinking for me. But Sidney." Grace cocks her head. "How is it you still can't fake smile for shit?"

"Get out of here. My fake smile is excellent."

"Sure. You keep telling yourself that." She grins. "Out of respect for you, I guess I won't hit on him."

"Do what you want. Noah and I are just friends and that's fine."

She watches me with interest, waiting for more.

I eventually settle on saying, "My life isn't the sort of situation most sane people want to be a part of."

"But you've dated, right? After everything with Ryan?"

"Not so much."

Her lips turn down at the edges. "That's sad."

"It's also because I'm reluctant to put myself out there. And I am working on that."

"Good." Her smile returns. "Oh my, God. Do you remember Adam Moore?"

"There's a name I haven't heard in a while. We spent a whole summer staring at that poor boy."

"Whatever happened to him?"

"Last time I saw him was senior prom," I say. "He and his boyfriend seemed happy."

She barks out a laugh.

Here's another thing I forgot—how Grace lets the happy out good and loud. Back in the day, her mom would drive her out at the start of the summer and stay a night. Then do the same when it was time for my cousin to go home. Those were the only occasions Grace would turn down the volume on her laugh. We used to debate which was worse—a dead mom or a shitty one. Both probably require immense amounts of therapy.

Grace's phone sits with its screen down on the table. A good idea for not getting distracted during a conversation. She picks up another book from the pile on the table. This time it's *I'll Be Gone in the Dark* by Michelle McNamara. My therapist might have a point with it being an obsession. "I know this one too," says Grace. "He used to give me so much shit for watching true crime."

"The ex-fiancé?"

She bares her teeth in a smile. "He said it was morbid and prurient. God, he used to go on at me. What do you think?"

"I think it's complicated."

"How so?"

"There're some valid lizard brain reasons why watching true crime feels good. I mean it helps us become more aware of danger and hopefully learn how to avoid it. We're educating ourselves, which can be useful. But then we also get to feel relieved that we're not the victim, you know?"

"That's kind of awful. What else have you got?"

I down some more coffee. "Well…I feel like it gives us the opportunity to feel compassion and fear and horror in a safe environment. Also, people love solving puzzles, so…"

"You've given this a lot of thought."

"Yeah. Of course, there are massive and complex issues around consent and financial compensation for victims and their families and the need to restrict the dramatization or romanticizing of these stories." I pause to take a breath. "Oof. Sounds like I am giving you a lecture. You will not be tested on this later."

"Keep going. I'm interested in what you have to say. Your life…your experiences…they're pretty damn unique."

"Mm."

She sits on the edge of her chair with her gaze locked on me. "Sidney, did you know his mom is talking to the documentary people?"

"No. But Dianne talking to them doesn't surprise me."

"She said a psychic told her it was all your fault. That you're the one who should be in prison. What do you think of that?"

I shrug. Because seriously, what is there to say?

"Come on," she says with an eager smile. "You must have some thoughts on it. How does it make you feel? And how do you think that strand of your hair got on the body?"

"He was my boyfriend. We touched and stuff. It got on him and then it got on her. They call it secondary transfer."

"Yeah, but—"

"Where did you hear that about Dianne?"

Grace pauses. "You know. Talk on social media."

"You're following it?"

"Some. I was curious about you. Is that a problem?"

"No. I guess not."

"It's just kind of wild, you know?" she asks. "You said it didn't surprise you she was talking to them. Why is that?"

"Um."

"Did you get along with her when you and Ryan were dating?"

My smile is all sorts of awkward. This conversation suddenly feels off. Invasive in some strange way. "We need ice cream. Can't have pancakes without ice cream. I am going to head down the street to buy some."

"Oh."

"Back soon."

I am not fleeing my house to escape my guest. Though it sure looks like it. Outside on the street, I can breathe a little easier and relax. Having someone in my space overnight is interesting. Grace and I might have been close as children. But we need to navigate this new relationship as adults. Guess it's going to take some time to feel comfortable with each other again. I might need to set boundaries about some subjects. Which is part of a healthy relationship and to be expected. Though I do wonder how long she's thinking of staying.

CHAPTER SEVEN

LIVING CLOSE TO AN ICE CREAM SHOP IS A BEAUTIFUL/ terrible thing. The constant temptation to buy everything and fall into a food coma for a hundred years is very real. You can't tell me Sleeping Beauty wouldn't have chosen it over pricking her finger on some stupid spindle.

I don't know when the small dog starts following me on the way back. Though his scent soon makes him hard to ignore. No idea what he's rolled in, but whoa. When I think about it…as stinky as he is, I would still take him over my other stalker. Her absence is something to be relished and enjoyed. The dog is small and fluffy. But it's hard to tell his breed beneath all the brown muck.

"Go home."

He sits his butt on the asphalt and cocks his head.

"You need to go home."

His bright eyes shoot to the pint in my hands before returning to my face. And the inference is obvious.

"No. This is my ice cream. You can't have any," I say in a stern voice. Then I resume walking. He waits a moment before following me again. I can hear the tapping of his nails against the pavement. This has to stop because a single house guest is more than enough. "Dogs are allergic to chocolate. I can't give you any. It would make you sick."

The little dude does not seem convinced. As if I would lie about something so important.

"It's not safe for you out here," I tell him over my shoulder. "You could get hit by a car or something. Whoever's supposed to be looking after you is doing a shitty job. I'd complain to management if I were you."

He gives me a doggy smile and falls into step beside me.

"Bad dog."

At this he stops and blinks. Like he actually seems taken aback by my words. Hurt even.

"Sorry," I say. "That was mean and unnecessary. I am sure you're a very good dog despite the smell. But you can't keep following me."

His big bright liquid eyes gaze up at me. If I ignore him, he might get bored and go home. We walk the rest of the way in silence. I have to admire his dedication to frozen desserts.

No idea how much dogs usually pant, but he seems to be doing a lot of it and the day is a warm one. He might need some water. In which case, hassling the nearest human makes sense. We reach the house, and I fish the front door key out of my pocket.

"You wait here, and I'll get you something to drink, okay?"

But the moment the door opens wide enough he dashes inside. He's just a streak of matted muddy fur disappearing underneath the couch and dashing through the dining room before making a move for the kitchen. My cousin's high-pitched shriek is ear piercing. Guess he startled her. I chase after the rampaging canine with ice cream in hand.

"Who the hell are you?" Noah's standing at the back door, holding the dog up in front of his face. "No collar."

I put the ice cream in the freezer and find a bowl to fill with water. "There isn't?"

He shakes his head.

"Shit."

"Not much meat on him either. Might have been living on the streets for a while."

"That thing stinks." Grace dramatically covers her nose with her hand. "Will you please get it out of here?"

"Guess I'll take him to the vet to get his chip read," I say, ignoring my dramatic dog-hating cousin.

Noah sets him down in front of the bowl of water and the dog starts lapping it up. "You can't put him in your car smelling like this."

"No," I agree.

"I'm out of here," says Grace, abandoning us and our new stinky friend to our fates.

Noah watches as the dog keeps drinking. "I've got to get to work. The fence is repaired for now. Enough to keep him in if you want to put him out back. I can help you wash him, but it wouldn't be until tomorrow."

"Thank you for the fence," I say. "What can I do for you?"

"Huh?"

"You keep doing things for me. I'd like to reciprocate."

"Don't worry about that," he says, dismissing the idea with a shake of his head. Like it's silly or something.

A drop of sweat traces a line down the side of his thick

neck. It's embarrassing how thoroughly such a small thing manages to derail my entire thought process. My life and the eternal quest for meaning and or forgiveness. None of it means anything compared to the fine line it leaves down his tattoo. I can almost taste the salt on my tongue. There I stand, staring at him with my mouth hanging open and… shit.

"Sid? Are you okay?"

"Um. Yeah. Yes." I give him the most fake-ass smile in my arsenal. "Don't worry about the dog. I've got this. No problem."

"This is a problem," I say with a sigh. "We have no idea who he belongs to?"

It took over an hour of me and the dog in the bathroom with both bottles of my expensive new salon-quality-sensitive organic shampoo and conditioner to get him clean. He now smells low key, like sea salt and lemon. A huge improvement. Though my hairbrush will never be the same. And let's not talk about the state of the bathroom. Grace hid in the spare room with the door shut the entire time. Coward. My cousin is apparently not a dog person. Waiting until Noah could help me with him tomorrow might have been the smarter move. But getting the dog checked out took precedence.

The local veterinarian, Doctor Jiya, gives me a smile. "No collar or chip makes it hard. We can do a search of local lost animal groups on social media and post about him on there, but…"

"He may have been dumped."

"Yes," she says. "You did a good job cleaning him up. But from the state of him, I'd say he's been on the streets for a while."

I nod.

"He's a terrier mix. One of his parents was probably a Westie. No idea what the other might have been. He's about three years old and has already been desexed, which is the good news. The bad news is he's probably due for some shots and in need of a good home."

The dog lies on the examination table on his back with his pink tongue hanging out as the good doctor gives him belly rubs. Dignity does not concern him. This happy behavior is a dramatic change from his mournful howling during bathtime. He keeps looking over at me to make sure I haven't disappeared. It makes my heart hurt for him.

"I can pay for the shots," I say.

"Great. There'll be a discount given the situation. Now how do you feel about giving him a home?"

"I've never looked after a dog before." I frown. "My grandmother was allergic. We had goldfish when I was growing up."

"You're doing well with him so far. It could be temporary. He might have escaped, and the owners could contact us wanting him back."

"But in the meantime, he needs a home."

"Yes," she says hopefully. "The local no-kill shelter is full, unfortunately."

Of course, he's now gazing adoringly at me with his big bright eyes. I highly doubt there's a single coherent thought happening inside his little head. Just vibes. And doubtless he looks this way at anyone with a proven history of bribing him with cheese. But it still stirs my cold dead heart. Not to get all woe is me, but I know what it's like to be abandoned.

"When else am I going to get the chance to be a single stay-at-home dog mom?"

"Who knew dogs needed so much stuff?"

Grace cocks her head later that afternoon. "I am not convinced they do."

We're sitting on the sofa watching the canine in question. He's blissfully asleep on his new navy tweed memory foam bed. He's wearing his matching navy leather and silver-studded collar. The stuffed toy duck he's curled up with doesn't match anything but does look cute as fuck. Which is why I've taken about a hundred photos of him. In other news, my renewed interest in shopping and photography are going great. Might be a good idea to start calming down on the spending, however.

"You can't just expect him to lie on the floor like an animal," I say. "And the dog boutique was having a sale."

"They don't call it a pet store?"

"Apparently not. There were sweaters and costumes for Halloween and everything."

Grace is more amused than impressed. "You're going to turn into one of those people who have a social media account for their pet, aren't you?"

"He might not even be staying. This is all temporary. I'm not even sure I want a dog."

"That why did you buy up half the store?"

"No comment."

She snorts.

An array of old photo albums are on the coffee table. It seemed like a good idea to divert her from further discussions about death and DNA and to help us reconnect. Grandma often carried around a camera. She'd take shots of things she wanted to sketch or paint. So there's plenty of scenery from the local area. But also, a lot of my cousin and me from our summers together. Pictures of us swimming and bowling and hanging out at the mall. Doing all of those normal everyday things. Guess my interest in photography comes from Grandma.

"What are you going to name him?" asks Grace. "You have to call him something."

"I don't know."

The dog opens an eyelid to check that I'm still sitting where he left me. He wags his tail exactly once, before going back to sleep.

"How about Fluffy?" asks Grace.

"No."

"Smelly? Stinky?"

"That was an unfortunate situation that has since been remedied," I say. "Which reminds me…I need to buy more shampoo."

"I gave the bathroom a wipe-over while you were out."

"You did?" I pause in surprise. "Thank you."

"You're welcome. But you can deal with the wet towels." Her smile is one-sided. "Saw the gym setup in the garage. The boxing bag and so on. Do you use it a lot?"

"Yeah." I hold up my hand and show her my knuckles. "I have calluses and everything. It's honestly been kind of therapeutic for me. A way to safely deal with any anger or general negative emotions."

Her gaze turns bitter, and she says, "We're not supposed to have those feelings."

"No. Women are not."

"Society wants us to smile and be pretty and nothing more." She takes a deep breath. "And what's the room at the back of the house? You use it for a study or something?"

"Something like that."

A line appears between her brows. Like she wants to ask more but is holding herself back. Setting boundaries with my cousin has been successful. I made it clear that I didn't want to talk about my ex or anything relating to that situation. Not that she knows about the contents of the war room, since the door is locked. But she's stopped pushing.

It's strange how discussing these things with Noah didn't put me on edge, while similar conversations with my cousin does. Guess I've spent more time with him recently. We have a level of trust between us. I don't want to spill the tea, be a fascinating case study, or a cautionary tale. All of those lenses have a bad habit of blurring the details that make me a living, breathing person. My relationship with friends and family should be different and deeper.

Though there's a small chance I am being overly sensitive. I don't know. It's an understandably sensitive topic.

Grandma and I talked about anything and everything. The cringe I experienced each and every time she sat me down to discuss sex as I was growing up. Because for some reason we had to have the conversation more than once. Guess aging hippies and arty types tend to be open to most things. It left me believing it's how things should be with people close to you.

"Tackle any more of your wedding deposits today?" I ask in a careful voice.

She wrinkles her nose. "Lost thousands on the dress. But managed to get the booking fee for the reception place refunded. They had another couple ready to take the date."

"That's great."

"Yeah." She frowns at her pale pink toenails. "It was going to be so beautiful. I had it all planned out."

"You'll make an amazing bride someday. But in the meantime, it's okay to grieve what was lost. I'm sorry you're going through this."

She tries to smile, but it doesn't quite stick. Her phone buzzes and she turns it over to check the screen. Then she swallows, gives me a smile, and changes the subject. Which is fair. We both have our sore spots worth respecting. "What do you normally do on a Friday afternoon? Have a glass of wine?"

"We can do that," I respond.

"And we need snacks."

"That's the best idea I've heard all day." I head into the kitchen to find the necessary supplies. Cheese and crackers and a bottle of white wine from the back of the cupboard. A shame I didn't think to put it in the fridge earlier. But this is exactly why we have ice cubes. "We should use Grandma's vintage wineglasses."

Grace follows me, leaning her shoulder against the doorframe. She seems uncomfortable again. I hope we get past this stage soon so we can relax around one another.

I hold up one of the glasses. "Check it out. Stem so thick

and heavy you could honestly clobber someone over the head with it."

"That's not a wineglass, it's a weapon," she says in awe.

"Right?"

"They're gorgeous. Mom was just so pissed she left you everything."

"Yeah." I sigh. "I asked if there was anything she wanted to remember her by, but…"

"It is what it is." Grace shrugs. "Why don't we invite hot neighbor over for a drink?"

"He's at work."

"You know his movements?"

"No. I mean, not really. But he's a chef, so…"

Her smile turns lascivious. "That's a damn shame he isn't around."

"Yeah."

"I was thinking he'd be perfect for a rebound hookup. What with me only being in town for a while and him living right next door."

"Always good to save on gas. So environmentally friendly, too."

"You don't really care, do you?" she asks. "I know I was teasing you earlier, but if you two are just friends I could really do with the dopamine."

She sure changed her mind quickly. The truth is, I mind to an alarming degree. Thoughts regarding someone else touching Noah make me want to scream and scratch stuff. Just go full-on harpy. But that's my bad luck. I'm saved from having to respond by the dog. He starts barking a moment before someone knocks on the front door. The little dude dislikes visitors, apparently. How nice that my new canine companion (temporary or otherwise) and I have things in common.

Grace gives me a bright smile. "I'll get it."

"Wait a minute." I follow her back into the lounge room, pick my phone up off the cluttered coffee table, and open the security camera app. "Just let me check…"

Meanwhile, she's walking toward the door with her hand outstretched. She slides back the chain and turns the deadbolt.

And there on my phone screen is a collection of people. One of whom has a big-ass camera held up to their face. What fuckery is this?

"Grace," I say. "Stop!"

But she doesn't. It's like it happens in slow motion. She looks back at me over her shoulder with a perfectly blank face while her hand turns the knob. The door swings open and shit. There they are. One of the podcasters from the new documentary with a cameraman and sound guy. All standing squished together on my front step.

Over on his bed, the dog jumps to attention and starts barking his head off. It's a heck of a noise.

"Sidney, we just have a couple of questions for you." The podcaster's friendly smile is all sharp teeth. "You didn't respond to our email or other attempts to contact you. This is your chance to tell your version of events. Surely you can see that's important?"

Grace stands with her back to the wall. Leaving a clear path between me and them.

"Let's sit down and have a conversation," the asshole yells to be heard over all the noise.

"Get off my property." I cover the space between us in an

instant and attempt to shut the door. Of course, he tries to stop me. "Move your foot."

"Hasn't Ryan suffered long enough? It's time for you to be honest about what really happened. How you were really involved in Briana's murder!"

With my hands hard against the back of the door, I kick at his big-ass sneaker with my bare foot. It takes one, two, three attempts to dislodge the asshole. But then the door finally slams shut. I turn the deadbolt and take a deep breath. And then another, because what a clusterfuck.

Grace stands nearby. Her mouth moves; however, no words come out. Like she doesn't know what to say.

I don't have that problem. "Why didn't you stop?"

"Sorry," she blurts out.

More banging on the door. Footsteps shuffle outside. The dog stands at my feet growling. He is not impressed with these shenanigans. Which makes two of us.

My heart hammers inside my chest. It's just the adrenaline pumping through me. They didn't get in or hear anything of interest from me. Everything is okay. However, they do now have fresh footage of me for their show.

But my cousin…there's something going on. She doesn't seem to want to meet my eyes.

"Grace, didn't you hear me?"

"I said I am sorry," she says. And then nothing more.

I take a deep breath and let it out slowly. "Okay. It's okay. Guess they could just as easily have sprung this on me at the grocery store or something."

Her shoulders drop.

"Why don't we get those glasses of wine and watch something on TV?" My smile is guarded and fake as can be.

But this time she doesn't seem to know the difference. "Sure, Sidney."

You learn a lot about a house after living in it for almost a decade. Which floorboards and steps tend to creak or squeak. Which sounds are normal, and which are an anomaly. The dog stays curled up on his bed in the corner of my room. Whatever nonsense I am up to at two in the morning doesn't interest him one iota. A sensible outlook on life. None of the lights are on, but I know my way around. Down the staircase and through the living room as quiet as can be. Go me in stealth mode. A ninja would be jealous.

Grace swears softly in the dining room. She sounds frustrated. The light from her phone is shining on the study door as she stands with her back to me. This week is giving real gain-a-dog, lose-a-cousin sort of vibes.

It's almost comical the way she jumps when I turn on the overhead light. How with wide eyes she spins to face me. Her phone is in one hand and a short knife in the other. Guess it's what she was trying to bust the lock with, but now she's holding it in front of her body for protection. Oof.

I don't say anything.

She licks her lips. "You're a really light sleeper."

"Yeah."

"I told you I was broke."

"That's why you opened the door to them," I say. "You're working for them. Have you been recording our conversations?"

"There's a release form I need you to sign."

"I should have been more suspicious about the pancakes and bathroom cleaning. Doing chores was never really your thing."

She snorts.

"I knew the timing was weird, you turning up here like this, and I still asked you to stay." I shake my head. "Get out of my house."

"You can't throw me out in the middle of the night."

"Of course I can."

"Grandma would—"

"Be fucking furious at you for this and you know it."

Her mouth is small and tight. But she doesn't bother trying to deny it. "You have to sign the release. I need the money. It's not like there's even anything that bad on there. What little you said was pretty rational, actually."

"Thanks," I reply drily. "That means a lot coming from you."

"The documentary's going ahead whether you like it or not, Sidney. And they're desperate for information on you. I don't know how many thousands they'd pay you for a proper interview. But they're not the only ones willing to hand over money. You're an idiot for not getting what you can out of it. For not at least countering their bullshit arguments."

"If you think it's such bull, why are you pointing that knife at me? Do you think I was involved in the killings?"

Nothing from her on this point. But what she does say is, "We're family. Signing the release is the least you can do."

"You really believe that, don't you?" I ask in wonder. "Get your shit and get out of my house."

CHAPTER EIGHT

MY COUSIN DOESN'T WASTE ANY TIME. NEITHER DO THE podcasters for that matter. Turns out they're not just in town doing the documentary. A new episode of their podcast drops the very next day when we're on our way back from Underhill State Park.

Muriel, Hana, and I have been there before for our mission. But it's reasonably close to town and worth another visit just to be safe. Nothing stood out to me, though. I don't remember anything in particular about the place.

Though today wasn't a complete waste. It was good to get out. And the dog is living his best life—going on walks and soaking up attention from everyone. We also spent quality time together. Just the four of us, with a strawberry and rhubarb pie that had the most amazing crust.

But back to the podcast we play on our way home.

Vermont doesn't seem to have any laws about recording someone. Whether it be an in-person conversation, over the phone, or electronic messaging. Consent from one of the parties involved sort of makes it legal, as I understand it. However, I had an expectation of privacy since the communication happened in my home. Which is why Grace wanted me to sign the release. Lack of it leaves the documentary makers open to a possible civil suit from me. Though certain federal laws could also kick in and further complicate things, apparently.

I don't know. I *think* that's how it all works. There hasn't been time to talk to my lawyer yet. So this information all comes courtesy of some middle-of-the-night internet searches. But the podcasters must basically agree with me since they don't play the recordings taken by Grace. They rely on her to repeat both the salient facts and insinuations.

A brief recitation of our childhood years kicks off the episode. All of those summers we spent together. It blows my mind how complete strangers could be interested in any of this. That they could be invested in the nonsense we did when we were eight. But they eventually reach my college years and the unraveling of my life, and so on.

"Sidney hasn't moved on from that poor woman's death or the court case," says Grace. "These events still very much dominate her life."

"In what way?" asks one of the podcasters.

Grace clears her throat. "Well, she's isolated herself and doesn't date, for starters."

"Do you think that's because she feels guilty?"

"I don't know if my cousin is guilty of anything," says Grace, speaking sense for a brief beautiful moment. "It could all just be an understandable reaction to the horrible things that happened to her."

"No shit," grumbles Muriel from the passenger seat.

"How else has it affected her?" asks the interviewer in his deathly serious voice.

"She's obsessed with true crime," says Grace. "Has books about it all over her house."

"Oh, come on." My fingers squeeze the steering wheel. "There were like a couple on the dining room table."

Hana winces. "And then there's your library in the study."

"Yeah, but she didn't see that, so it doesn't count."

"True."

The dog gives an almighty huff from the backseat of the Subaru. I take it to be in support of me. Hana is giving him ear scratches, another thing he approves of mightily.

"What are her feelings regarding the documentary?" asks the interviewer. "When we set out to do this project, it was important to us to represent all sides of this story. With respect for the victim or possible victims coming first and foremost, of course. We've tried contacting Sidney numerous times and never received a reply. And when we knocked on her door recently, she was extremely hostile."

"That was surprising," interjects another dude. "The violence of her reaction was almost unhinged. How many times did she kick you? Three? Four?"

"Go fuck yourself." I shake my head. "You tried to invade my home and then stopped me from shutting the door."

Muriel just sighs.

"Yeah. I agree, Steve," says the first guy. "It's as if she wants to stop us and suppress this story for some reason. To hide the truth and the careful and balanced reporting we're working so hard to reveal to the authorities, the general public, and of course you—our loyal listening audience. If you're new to our show, don't forget to hit that subscribe button. Updates about this case are coming in all the time and you don't want to miss out!"

"You sure don't. We appreciate you being here today, Grace," says Steve. "What else can you tell us?"

My cousin sighs. The woe is real. "Sidney can be secretive and hard to read. We're very close. So close. But like I said before, while my cousin used to be outgoing, these days she's more of a private person. Someone who finds it hard to trust. Even me."

"Things really changed inside of her during those late teen years, didn't they? Around the time when she started college and met Ryan. It's as if who she was as a person was somehow altered, and not for the better. Did she perhaps experience an event that turned her to the dark side?"

"I don't know about that. But her ease with violence certainly surprised me," answers Grace. "Having a punching bag in the house and all. We weren't raised to be aggressive like that. I mean, she has calluses on her hands from hitting things, for goodness' sake."

Grandma bought me my first pepper spray. But whatever.

"Were you ever frightened in your cousin's presence?" asks the first interviewer. The one whose name we don't know. "Scared for your safety?"

"I want to say no," answers my cousin with a waver in her voice. "But it would be a lie."

"It's okay, Grace. Take your time. We know this must be upsetting for you."

Hana scoffs. "Is this lying traitorous hyperbolic bitch actually crying?"

"She was a theatre kid for a while," I say.

"What I think is important here is that I believe Sidney

is looking for the bodies of the other missing women," continues Grace.

Shit.

"Why do you think that?" asks Steve.

"On her dining table, I saw a printout of an article about cadaver dogs. How they're able to detect dead bodies and then signal to their trainers. Stuff like that."

"Are you thinking what I'm thinking?" The excitement in the podcaster's voice is palpable.

"That there's a proven history of criminals involving themselves in their cases? Yes indeed," says Steve. "We've often seen these sorts of people insert themselves into an investigation to enable them to feel important and clever. While allowing them to relive some of the thrill they experience when killing, of course, by talking about what happened with detectives."

"Kemper used to hang out at a cop bar. Bundy liked to pose as one!"

"Not to forget the Golden State Killer actually worked as one for several years. These sorts of people are often attracted to officials and the power they wield. What an amazing development. And dare I say another strong indicator that Sidney was far more involved in the death of Briana Petersen than she's admitted. Just as we suspected." Steve's voice is as excited as can be. "Or is she researching how investigators might find the hidden bodies?"

The second podcaster oohs and ahhs. "You could very well be right."

"Or it could mean she's trying to help," says Grace, sounding perturbed by their spin. "By trying to find the bodies of the other missing women. Which is what someone caught up in this horrible situation might do, right?"

"But we know that Ryan didn't have anything to do with those other women going missing," says Steve. "The local police have said he's not a person of interest."

"What if they're wrong?" asks Grace. "I know there's at least one online true crime community trying to find a connection."

Which is not what the podcasters want to hear. "What else can you tell us about your cousin, Grace?"

Guess she sees dollar signs flash before her eyes. Because it takes her a moment, but she comes up with more. "I also sensed that Sidney had a lot of animosity toward Ryan's mom. She said she still does therapy once a month when she needs it. But she seemed to have a lot of unresolved negative feelings around his family."

"That doesn't surprise us. Dianne has been a bastion of strength to her son over the years. Her righteous anger and dedication to seeking justice for Ryan remains fierce and undaunted. The access she's given us during the making of this podcast and the upcoming documentary are just…I don't know how we would have done it without her."

"That's right, Mike," says the other dude.

"Yeah. But she thinks he's innocent because a psychic told her, right?" asks Grace. "It's not exactly scientific evidence. Next you'll be judging Sidney based on her aura or birthstone or something."

"The case is extremely complex and involved," answers Steve in a rush. "We don't want to diminish other people's spiritual beliefs. Thank you so much for coming in today,

Grace. Your insights on your cousin have been invaluable and we sure appreciate the access you granted us."

They move on to telling listeners where they can buy Team Ryan and Team Sidney tees. Then they announce they'll be interviewing my old hairdresser. She has a lot to say, apparently. Give me strength. The voices cut off as Hana stops the podcast and silence fills the vehicle.

"Wonder if they'll talk to the person who does your waxing," says Muriel in her usual dry tone.

"Of course, it was the repeated pain of getting my pubic hair ripped out that tipped me over the edge. You know that, right?"

Hana snorts. "Something had to send you to the dark side."

"What absolute baloney." Muriel shakes her head. "Balanced reporting my ass. They're a pair of hacks."

"Your cousin sucks, by the way. Hey, Rodney? Stanley? Walter?" Hana shakes her head. "The doggo isn't reacting to any of them. We'll figure out your name eventually. Don't worry."

"He might not be staying," I remind her. And as for Grace... "I knew the timing was weird. Her turning up like that. Never should have offered to let her stay. At least if she'd been at a motel, I would have had some distance and time to think about the things she was asking and maybe piece it together."

Hana winces. "Not really sure you should drag yourself for not being paranoid enough."

"I completely forgot the stuff about cadaver dogs was on the table. There was a bunch of bills and stuff and...yeah."

"So people know we're searching," says Hana. "There's no reason it necessarily changes anything."

"I feel like such an idiot."

"Let me know when she moves on from the self-pitying stage," says Muriel. "I always find that boring."

Hana smiles. "Calling yourself an idiot seems harsh."

"Idiot adjacent?" I ask.

"Yeah. I'll let you have that one."

"Thanks. You're probably right about it not changing anything," I say after some thought. "My reputation was already shitty. Maybe it won't make much of a difference."

Muriel makes a humming noise. "I guess we'll see."

"Time for a change of topic. Are you still thinking of going to Noah's housewarming drinks tomorrow night?" asks Hana. "For what it's worth, I think you should."

"Hold on," inserts Muriel. "Why didn't I hear anything about this? I was going to invite you back to bingo."

"Bingo was great," I say.

"No. Go to Noah's." Muriel takes off her glasses to give them a clean. "I did another deep dive of his online life. Just for fun."

I raise my brows. "Your definition of fun worries me sometimes."

"The point is, apart from some questionable life choices in his early twenties, the man seems like one of the good ones. I approve of him."

No point repeating that we're just friends. They're already aware. More than.

"I like him too," says Hana. "What do you think, Willard? Roger? August? He's wagging his tail. I think August is a winner. You're so cute, Auggie. The cutest dog on the whole backseat of the car with his head currently resting on my leg."

I laugh. "That's pretty specific."

"I want him to feel seen. To be perceived. How do you feel about Auggie?"

"Hmm. It's the month when I found him. Or he found me," I say with a smile. "I think it works. Auggie it is."

"And you're going to the party?"

"Sure," I say with almost no doubt. "Why not?"

Music and chatter are flowing out of the front door of the small brick bungalow next door the next evening. I've never been in any of the neighboring houses before. What a momentous occasion. Back in the days of yore you would turn up to parties with a six-pack of beer along with your hopes and dreams. But a bottle of wine and a dose of reality seems more adult. Noah asked me to attend. Everything is going to be fine. Hiding away has been my norm for so long that there are bound to be nerves. But I can definitely do this. As in go out and get a life.

I wear a pair of blue jeans, and a new black square-neck knit tank with sandals. It took me forever to get my cat's-eye liner right. Thank fuck for online tutorials.

No idea how many people it takes to run a restaurant. But there are four sitting in the room, including Noah. He told me it would basically just be people from work because those are the only people besides me that he's met in town so far.

The house has an open-plan kitchen/dining/living space. A couple of packing boxes sit in a corner. There are a couple of tan sofas, a wooden coffee table, and a glass four-seater dining table with a record player sitting on top. No art or photos on the wall. Not yet. His residence is a work in progress.

Just the sight of him makes the ball of anxiety in my belly ease. There'll be no need for a fire this winter. His gaze warms me just fine. Which is not the thought of a friend, but I am doing my best here. He's wearing black jeans with a black tee and boots. I have to force myself not to swoon. I really need to stop dreaming about this man being naked. For both our sakes.

"Hey," he says, getting to his feet. "You made it."

"Yeah."

He smiles, and I am not imagining how he stands closer than necessary. His back is to the room, blocking me from view, like he's giving me a minute to adjust or something. And I appreciate it, but I am okay.

"What happened with the dog?" he asks. "I haven't heard how things went at the vet."

"Auggie is at home asleep on the couch. He doesn't have a chip, so we're waiting to hear if anyone is missing him. But for now he's staying with me."

"Is that so?" His smile really is all things fair and good in this world. I hand him the bottle of wine and he asks, "Can I get you a glass of that?"

"Sure."

"Let me introduce you quickly."

When he steps aside, three sets of eyes are watching us with interest. A beautiful Black woman with her braids in a low bun is sitting beside a young white man with piercings. And on a low wooden stool is a woman with olive skin and a shaved head wearing an amazing vintage-style dress. Talk about serving cunt.

"This is Ivy, Logan, and Jade," he says. "And this is Sidney."

Noah hasn't told them about me. This much is made obvious quickly. But he stands at my side with a determined smile. The dawning recognition on Jade's face is distinctly horrified while Logan's is blessedly oblivious. And as for Ivy, she knows who I am but keeps a careful smile on her face. Which I appreciate. I wonder how far I would have to move to get away from this. From being known. Though the idea of running does kind of piss me off. The thing is, with the documentary coming out on a major streaming service, nowhere might be far enough now.

"You're the neighbor?" says Jade, voice heavy with disbelief.

"Which is not a problem." Noah rests his hand on the small of my back.

Logan's gaze jumps around the room. "What's going on?"

No one says anything for a minute. Then Ivy says in an even tone, "She used to date a guy who killed a girl. You were probably too young to pay attention. What was it…nine or ten years ago?"

I nod. "About that."

"Wow," says Logan with wide eyes.

Ivy's smile is determined. "All of the smokers are out back. Come and join us, Sidney."

"Thanks," I say.

"I remember," says Logan like genius is dawning on him. "A bunch of women went missing. Mom cut her hair and stopped jogging alone or listening to music when she was out."

This is awkward. But it's also to be expected. As long as I stay in this city, being recognized and having conversations like this are going to happen. I'm determined to keep living my life and making my peace with it. Noah wants me here and that's what matters.

"It was terrifying." Jade's gaze is flat and unfriendly. "I knew one of the women who went missing. We were friends."

I open my mouth to say I am sorry. The most useless three words in existence. But alas, I'm too slow.

"Sid had nothing to do with it," says Noah. "Why don't we talk about something else?"

"Of course she had something to do with it. A hair from her head was found on a murder victim."

"You're right," I say before Noah can intercede on my behalf again. Confrontation sucks. But there's no avoiding this. "I was dating the person who hurt those women. When I was nineteen, I had awful fucking taste in men. Just the absolute worst. I couldn't see through his bullshit and lies. I'm sorry about your friend. But I didn't know what he was doing and I wasn't involved in the murder or kidnapping of any of those women."

Jade shakes her head. "And we're just supposed to take your word for that? At the very least he was able to hide for longer amongst us because of people like you."

"She made a shit choice," says Ivy. "But that monster was a smart good-looking boy from a seemingly nice family. You can't tell me if it hadn't been her, it wouldn't have been someone else."

Jade is not happy.

This is the point where I would normally back down. Shut my mouth and hide. But running from this hasn't gotten me anywhere. And it doesn't help anyone. "I am sorry you're hurting, Jade. I really am. But I am not the person who hurt you."

The woman just sits there and seethes.

Keeping my mouth shut might have been wiser. I think I just set a new land speed record for trashing a party's vibe. "Maybe I should um…"

"No," says Noah, determinedly.

"They're making a documentary about it, aren't they?" asks Logan, seemingly oblivious to the angst in the room. "A big group of the people involved are booked for dinner Wednesday."

Ivy nods.

"This is my house." Noah's jaw is set. "She's my guest too, Jade. You don't have to like her. I like her enough for both of us. But we need to drop this and talk about something else."

My heart swells to twice its normal size. This cannot be healthy. But I don't think I've been this excited about someone saying they like me since I was sixteen. It's all I can do to keep a stupid smile off my face. And this is so not the time or place for it.

"Fuck you, Noah," says Jade, grabbing her jacket and heading for the door.

The thing is…you can't tell someone how to grieve. How to feel about something so difficult. There are few things worse than losing someone and there's no closure for family and friends of the missing. In her position I might have reacted exactly the same. I honestly don't know.

Ivy blows out a breath but says nothing.

"Should I try and talk to her?" asks Noah.

"No." Ivy shakes her head. "Leave it with me."

"That was awkward as fuck." Logan raises his hand. "Can I say something? I don't understand wings."

"As in chicken wings?" asks Ivy with her brows drawn tight. "Are you serious? They're delicious. What's there to understand?"

I cock my head. "Yeah. Me neither."

"It's just skin and bone," says Logan. "There's no meat, right?"

"No," I say. "Never made sense to me."

Ivy blinks at us. "Delicious skin that's been marinated before being cooked to a golden crisp. How can you fail to appreciate that?"

"They're just good." Noah frowns down at me. You would think I insulted his firstborn or something. "Wings are good."

"Okay," I say.

"You're saying that just to appease me, aren't you?"

"Yes. Can I have that glass of wine?" I ask. "And please make it a large."

His gaze skips to the door, reminded of the recent trials and tribulations. No sign of Jade and I highly doubt she's coming back. Then he gives me the fakest smile in all of time and space and says, "You got it."

CHAPTER NINE

I HEAD HOME AT TEN. THE NEIGHBORHOOD IS QUIET, AS IT usually is on Sunday nights. There's an occasional hum from a car on the nearby road and the hoot of an owl perched high in a tree. Seven or so vehicles are parked on the street, care of the party. Though one, a dark sedan, is further down the way. Not that it actually matters. My brain would just rather think about random inconsequential shit as opposed to recent events.

Noah and I exchanged exactly a dozen words during the rest of the night. "Can I get you another drink?" "Is everything okay?" "See you later."

I don't need him to hover. But it feels like he was avoiding me and that sucks. Though maybe I'm overthinking it. I really hope I am.

The front door key is in my jeans pocket. My front porch isn't a big space. Just a couple of steps, a short wooden bench seat, and a planter full of white daisies. A small attempt at fitting into the neighborhood and appearing welcoming. Apart from the light above the door and another inside above the dining table, my house sits alone in darkness.

Logan leaves the party next. Shouting and laughter follow

him out the door. I see him raise his hand in farewell before climbing into a battered old Jeep. The sedan parked down the street comes to life as I slide the key in the lock. It cruises past with dark tinted windows. Which is when Auggie starts scratching at the door from inside.

"I'm coming," I say, putting myself between him and freedom. "Hi there, my friend. How was your night?"

His butt wiggles and he gives me a big doggy grin as I lock us safely inside. As for the question about how his night went, the answer would be great, apparently. What is not so great is the velvet throw pillow he viciously attacked and gutted. Fluffy balls of filling are spread across the living room floor.

"But I bought you toys," I say, deeply aggrieved. "Why choose violence?"

Auggie wags his tail in a manner I can only describe as joyous or elated. Hard to be angry with someone who's so damn happy to see you. Even if he does kill the décor for fun.

I take him out back and wait while he sniffs various places. He eventually settles for peeing on the base of the red maple. One of his favored spots. Then he trots back inside and curls up on his bed in the corner of the living room. Guess he doesn't want to come up to my room tonight.

It's good that he feels comfortable and doesn't need to shadow me. I read a couple of articles on settling in a new dog. How to avoid causing them unnecessary anxiety. A calm and happy dog lives a longer life.

Having another heartbeat in the house has been nice. There's a small chance I would be devastated if his previous owners showed up now.

When someone knocks on the door, he raises his head to

bark exactly once before going back to sleep. I check the security camera on my phone and open the door. We just said good night not five minutes ago. Him being here makes me nervous. Same goes for the heavy frown on his face.

"Noah."

"We need to talk," he says in this gravelly voice. "Can I come in?"

I nod and step back.

He closes the door behind him, stares down at me, and says, "This isn't working for me."

"You mean being friends with me, don't you?"

"Yes."

My stomach drops straight through the floor. "Okay."

"I know this is…it's not…shit." His hands curl into fists. Like he's holding in some big feelings. Something which is definitely going around right now.

Not to be melodramatic, but a dagger through the heart would hurt less. And not some skinny stiletto either. One of those big-ass hunting knives. "Tonight was awkward with Jade, and you have to work with her. It makes sense that you would need to keep that relationship as friendly as possible."

His brows draw tight together. "Yeah."

"What I am trying to say is that I understand."

"You do?"

I nod like a bobblehead doll. "I mean your work culture involves socializing sometimes and obviously—"

"Sid, this has nothing to do with what happened tonight."

"It doesn't?"

"No."

Forget the hunting knife. The man has harpooned me in the

heart. Hearing he doesn't want to be friends because of me and not the shitty situation that is my life is a whole new hellscape. As soon as he leaves, I'm going to hurl myself into the nearest abyss and/or suitably deep chasm. Then I am going to messy cry.

He cocks his head. "What are you talking about?"

"You don't want to be friends."

"No. It's not working."

"Right. So that's what I am talking about."

He steps closer and says, "You don't get it."

This is when I start frowning too. Because I'm not sure how much more I can take without bursting into tears. Something I do not want to happen. Please leave the tatters of my pride.

Which is when he takes my head in his hands and presses his mouth against mine. Then kisses me. His lips are firm and warm and oh so insistent. Like nothing else matters. His tongue teases my upper lip, and I open for him. Of course I do. He tastes of the wine we've been drinking. My body comes alive as my brain spins in dizzy circles. Having his tongue in my mouth and him holding me tight is heaven. All of the heat of him pressed up against me. It's not what I was expecting, but it's exactly what I need.

His pupils are blown, his eyes dark as night, when he pulls back. He licks his lips and smiles at me with hunger enough to make my knees weak. No one's ever looked at me the way he does. And his hands grasp me firmly—like he's worried I might try to slip away. Of which there is not a single fucking chance. Not in this lifetime.

"This is what I am talking about," he says.

"Huh." I think the situation over for all of a second. "Guess you have to get back to the party."

"Not if you don't want me to."

"I really don't want you to."

"Okay."

Such a simple thing to reach past him and lock the door. To take him by the hand and lead him upstairs to my bedroom. It's all shadows and moonlight up there. The perfect setting for what I have in mind. His cologne smells of sage and salt and it goes straight to my head. I want his scent on my skin and on my sheets. To be able to walk into this room and know he's been here.

"Look at me, Sid." He stops at the foot of the bed. "We can do as little or as much as you want. I'm in no rush. Just happy to be here."

It's a sweet sentiment. But I slip my feet out of my sandals and pull my top over my head. I can feel his gaze on my lace bra. My fingers are fumbling with the button and zipper of my jeans when he falls to his knees. He pushes the denim down and helps me step out of them. Then his big hands grasp my ass and draw me close. He nuzzles my belly button and the waist of my briefs. Seems I am not alone with the weird wanting-to-smell-him thing. Because his face is pressed against me and he's breathing in deep. A hand eases between my thighs. Fingertips brushing lightly back and forth over the soaked crotch of my panties.

The man is such a fucking tease. Shame on him.

Being this turned on is burning me up inside. Both my heart and my lungs are working hard. To finally be able to touch him is amazing. I am obsessed with the thick strands of his hair and the smooth skin of his face. His wide shoulders and strong neck. Never before have I been as fascinated by someone's body.

I want to climb all over him, to touch and taste. To learn him as well as I know myself.

As he rises to his feet, he grabs the back of his tee and drags it off over his head. So much beautiful bare skin. I kind of regret not turning on the light. He toes off his shoes and pulls off his socks and thank fuck we're finally down to his pants. His black jeans are soon tossed aside and this is like every birthday present at once. My hands in his hair and his mouth on mine. The hard length of his dick pressing against my belly.

He easily has my bra unhooked, straps sliding down my shoulders. Talk about skills. There's the slight sting of his stubble on my neck. Then the nip of his sharp teeth making me gasp. The way he has me aching and wanting. More and more and more.

"Tell me what you want," he says.

"I want you in me."

"We can do that."

"Now."

His smile is all sharp teeth.

Weird time to be thinking of my grandma. But I do want to thank her for training me to always have protection on hand. No matter how improbable an encounter might be. And it's been a long ten years. I crawl across the mattress reaching for the bedside table. And he follows, dragging his tongue up the back of my thigh, sending frissons of pleasure up my spine. Then his fingers hook in the sides of my underwear and start dragging them down. He lightly bites my ass cheek and whoa.

Giving up having sex with other people never seemed like a big deal. Sex was nice, but I didn't need it. Having someone so close to me didn't necessarily appeal. But no one told me it could be like this. What have I been missing all these years?

With a sex-addled brain, it's a trick to get the box of condoms open. My breath is stuttering and my hands are shaking. I have seen puzzles less complicated than this shit.

"Let me help you," says Noah, taking it from me.

I roll onto my back as he tears open the cardboard. In no time at all he's rolling a condom down the length of his cock. Thank goodness my gaze has adjusted to the low lighting. Because missing this sight would be a shame. Not getting to see him towering over me like a god. To have him kneeling between my spread legs with his hair disheveled and his dick hard. I'd write the man bad poetry if I only had the words. It's both too much and not enough—the want to crawl beneath his skin and show him my darkest parts.

He shoves his hand through his hair, pushing it back from his face. "I'm going down on you."

"No. Come here."

"You have no patience."

And he's not wrong. But he does as asked, stretching his big body out over mine. The heat coming off him is wild. To have his smooth skin and muscles and dusting of chest hair within easy reach is sublime. I wrap my legs around him good and tight. There's no hesitation. No second thoughts.

He takes his weight on one arm and positions the wide blunt head of his cock against me. His mouth takes mine in a fevered kiss as he pushes in slowly. It's an indescribable sort of ecstasy. The intimacy of being here with him and having him inside me. I moan and he growls and presses his forehead against mine. We're our own small safe world here on this bed. This is everything.

"Fuck me," he says, his voice deep and raw and real.

When his hips rest against mine, I press my nails into his shoulders just a little. Just enough to test him. And his feral grin answers all of my questions. He's every bit as overexcited and hanging on by a thread as me. Oh so slowly he pulls out, torturing us both. It's like he's lighting me up from inside. His heavy length pushes back in again, taking me over. My whole body is focused on the friction. Each and every nerve ending in me wide the fuck awake.

The warm palm of his hand cups my breast, molding and learning the shape. His clever fingers toy with the hard nipple. Sweat is already beading on my skin. I want to breathe him in and memorize him to the bone. Tie him to my bed and keep him here forever. It's not like me to be so jealous. But the emotions he's stirring are beyond my control.

His hand wanders down my side, taking my ass cheek in a firm grip. All the better to fuck me into the mattress. And I dig my heels in, urging him on. Harder and faster. Tension winds me tighter, the ache becoming louder and more insistent. I raise my hips to meet him again and again. Sensation streaks down my spine and yes. My hands grasp at his shoulders, holding him to me.

When the orgasm hits me, the whole world goes away. It's like I am floating in darkness, but there's nothing to fear. My body is wrapped around his. My sex squeezing him tight and keeping him deep. His hips buck against me time and again. Then he buries his face in my neck with a groan when he finishes. He tries to climb off me and I grunt in displeasure and hold on tighter. And he gives in and gives me his weight.

This moment should never end. We should always be on my bed. A tangle of limbs and a sticky sweaty mess.

"I am getting off you," he mumbles. "Any minute now."

"That's an awful idea. Why would you want to do that?"

He raises his head, cracks open one eyelid, and gives me a long look. "We're not getting much sleep for a while, are we?"

"No," I say with a smile.

Happiness and me don't usually have much in common. I am not sure I trust it. Though maybe I'm just not used to it. Which is not to say good dick can cure all evils—but it sure does help. And this is exactly what I am staring into space and thinking when the smoke alarm in the kitchen starts screaming.

"Shit, shit, shit."

The remains of the butter I put in the frying pan is an ominous black sludge. I turn off the stove and grab a dish towel to try and disperse the smoke. Opening the window would also help. Something I am busy doing when Noah enters the room, pulling his tee on over his head. He assesses the situation in no time, moves the overheated pan to a cooler section of the cooktop, and turns on the range hood.

"Did you burn yourself?" he asks, gaze running over me.

"No." My face is aflame with embarrassment, however. And the slice of bread I put in the bowl with the egg, milk, vanilla, and cinnamon mix is as soggy as can be. I have seen a swamp hold itself together better than this. "I was going to make breakfast."

"French toast, huh?"

"Yeah. But I got distracted."

"It happens. What were you thinking about?"

"I'd rather not say." I am not still blushing redder than a baboon's ass. That's someone else who looks disturbingly like me.

The way he just grins.

"Oh, my god. Your ego…I could have been thinking about baby ducks."

"You mean ducklings?"

"Yes. Though you knew what I meant, so the words worked and there was no need to correct me."

He nods. "You're right. I apologize. And baby ducks are pretty great."

"Damn right they are. Fluffy little miracles of nature."

I'm wearing a tank and a pair of pajama pants. While he's back in his black jeans with the top button undone. All of the hard lines of him in the morning sun is like a work of art. The stubble on his jaw and his dark mussed hair. He stretches and his tee slides up some. The line of hair leading down from his belly button disappearing into his pants sure is tempting. It's like a siren song. So damn hard to look away from.

"This is just like the time I got punched in the face during training because I thought I heard your car coming down the street."

He narrows his eyes on me. "You said you didn't remember what distracted you."

"I was hardly going to admit it, was I?"

"Hmm." He smiles and looks around. "Where's your dog this morning?"

"Auggie is busy sunbathing in the backyard. He has no job. He doesn't even pay taxes. Life for him is good."

Without a word, Noah backs me up some, grabs my hips, and sits me on the counter. A sweet single perfect kiss is placed on my forehead. Just the one. Then he places my cup of coffee in my hand before turning to make his own. And as soon as he's caffeinated, he takes over cooking us breakfast. Which is probably for the best.

"I'm usually competent in the kitchen," I say, taking a sip. "Setting things on fire is not the norm. Just so you're aware."

"Okay."

Good to be able to have this time with him. It's almost ten o'clock on a Monday. But my work is flexible, and I'm ahead with my hours. Noah being here is everything. True happiness would be waking up to this every morning. Him in my bed and making himself at home in my house. I haven't lived with anyone in a very long time. Not since Grandma. How weird would it be to not be alone?

And talk about getting ahead of myself. Time to enjoy the moment and be content in the now. There's no need to define this situationship or whatever it might be. Though I do wonder if we're officially dating. It sort of feels like we might be. Hard to trust my judgment, however, given the only serious boyfriend I had turned out to be a psycho killer.

Noah has the frying pan back in action and things cooking in no time. French toast turning a golden brown. Plates, silverware, and maple syrup ready and waiting. He really is a professional. You can see it in the expert way he wields a spatula. When he cuts another thick slice of bread (Grandma believed in buying whole loaves of bread), it's obvious how comfortable he is with a knife in his hand.

"Let's talk about us," he says out of nowhere. Just basically picking a topic of conversation out of the clear blue sky.

"Us?"

"Yeah." The man doesn't even make eye contact with me. Just carries on cooking like we're discussing the weather. "I like having sex with you, Sid. Do you like having sex with me?"

"Um. Yes?"

"You're not sure?"

"No," I amend hastily. "It's a definite. I very much enjoy having sex with you."

"Great. I thought so. But it's always good to check." He downs some coffee. "I would prefer if we were exclusive. You good with that?"

I nod.

"Now even with me trying to slow down, my work hours can be kind of hectic. One of the pitfalls of the job, unfortunately," he says. "How often ideally do you see us getting together? And by getting together I don't mean just fucking. Though fucking can of course be included. But talking to you, hanging out with you, that's important to me too, okay?"

"Wow." I stare at him in wonder. "You're so emotionally mature and relationship literate."

He just waits.

"I don't know what to say."

"This is new. We can figure out what works for us as we go. I know you're used to having space. And what with us living next to each other…I just want to be careful not to wear out my welcome." He tips his chin at me. "What are you thinking?"

"Honestly?"

"Of course."

"That I have years of celibacy to make up for and it's highly unlikely you're going to wear out your welcome anytime this century."

"But you'll tell me if you feel that changing, right?" he asks.

"I do. I mean…I will. Yes."

"Good."

He's so pretty when he smiles. A sight guaranteed to make my brain go to a galaxy far, far away. How he woke up my libido and shook up my life when he moved into the neighborhood. My world has changed more in the last month than it has in the last decade.

I am about to pour my heart out and tell him all of this when my canine house guest starts barking. Auggie races in through the open back door, making a mad dash for the front of the house. Noah takes the frying pan off the heat and follows with a frown.

My cell is in the next room on the dining room table. Just another sign of my lust-addled mind. Normally I would never have my connection to the security cameras out of reach. I jump down off the counter. This feels bad—whatever it is. And I seem to have developed a sixth sense for this shit over the years.

Auggie is busy growling when Noah swears and says, "Baby, there's a news crew filming on your front lawn."

CHAPTER TEN

THE PHONE IS RINGING. IT'S AN UNKNOWN NUMBER AND the timing sure is uncanny. I wouldn't normally answer. Just let it go to voicemail. But whatever is happening out front has got me distracted for the second time today. There are texts from Muriel on screen too. Asking me to call her urgently. What the heck is going on?

I answer the call. "Hello?"

"Will you accept charges for a call from Vermont Regional Correctional Facility?" asks a robotic voice.

He's never called me before. Not once in all these years. Those creepy letters arrive now and then, but they've been his sole means of communication. But he is bound to be the cause of whatever is going on right now. It's a definite. And the way fury fills me from head to toe at the thought. I don't even hesitate in my reply. "Yes."

"Your call will be subject to recording and monitoring."

Noah is busy drawing the curtains on the front windows and giving pats to Auggie. Trying to calm him down. The good boy is not happy about people hanging outside his home talking nonsense. Which is a sentiment we strongly share.

"Sidney," says the horribly familiar voice. And he sounds so fucking happy with himself. Just so very pleased. "How nice to talk to you. What's it been…ten years?"

"About that." Hearing my ex's low amused laugh sends a shiver down my spine. It makes my skin crawl. I hate him with everything in me and I don't care if it's healthy or not. "Ryan, how did you get this number?"

Noah's head snaps around at my mention of the name and there's a sudden wariness in his eyes. All of which is absolutely valid. I am not sure I should be giving my ex the time of day. It is in fact most likely an awful fucking idea. The worst I've had in a long time.

"What have you done?" I ask.

"Me? How could I have done anything? You're forgetting I'm still stuck in jail."

"Then why are you calling? Why now?"

"So many questions." He sighs. "It's important to me, for my spiritual and personal growth, to tell you that I forgive you."

My eyebrows reach for the sky. "You forgive me?"

"Yes," he continues. "Whatever demons forced you to carry out these terrible deeds are your own to deal with. I see that now. As much as I loved you, it was wrong of me to try and help you cover up your crimes."

"Your *love* almost killed me."

"Attacking you was a momentary lapse of reason on my part. Something I very much regret."

"Do you really think there's a chance they'll drop your charges to accessory and time served?"

"Anything is possible through the power of prayer. My therapist has also helped me understand myself and be a better, more empathetic person. To prepare for my return to the world and life outside of prison," he says. "Prayer and therapy are how I turned my life around and learned to accept the unfortunate role I played in enabling you."

"Enabling me?" I shake my head. "How many hours did you sit in your cell rehearsing this speech?"

"Sidney, I don't expect you to understand. But I found God and—"

"Oh, yeah? Where was he hiding? Behind the sofa?"

Noah pushes aside the curtain and checks on whatever is happening out front. The man is now as unhappy as the dog. Though he's doing a lot less growling.

"Don't interrupt me, please," says Ryan, an edge coming into his voice for the first time. "Hearing your name mentioned on the morning news made me realize some things. That this violence and corruption…this evil in your soul is a disease. One that's sure to catch up with you sooner rather than later."

"Okay."

"It saddens me that you've spent all these years alone."

"Been listening to the podcast, have you?" I ask. "They sure are your fan boys."

"Though perhaps isolating yourself was safest for the general public. You abstained for so long, I hoped perhaps you'd changed. But apparently not."

This is all such bullshit. He's giving me nothing useful. And the chances this conversation is going to wind up in the documentary are right up there. I put the call on speaker and start searching my name online.

"I know your grandmother was a just and peaceful woman," says Ryan. "Who tried to raise you to be a decent person."

"Do not talk about her."

"It gives me hope that one day you'll seek forgiveness and admit to the terrible things that you've done. But I wanted you to know, there is nothing but love and compassion in my heart for you, Sidney."

"Thanks. That really means a lot coming from you."

"Aren't you going to congratulate me on my engagement?" he asks. "Being in a stable healthy relationship with a good woman has really helped to ground me. I'm so excited about our future together. The idea of starting a family."

He prattles on as I scroll through a news feed. There's a photo of a luxury hatchback parked in a woodland area surrounded by crime scene tape. One of the car doors is open and various official-looking people are standing around. Some of them wear police uniforms. The article says the owner of the vehicle is missing, though no names have been released yet. Nothing about a body being found. There's obviously plenty of rumors going around, however, for reporters to be standing outside my house already. My history with Ryan has to be the sole link between me and the story about this vehicle. I mean, what else could it be?

This cannot be happening again. Women going missing and the community living in fear. The way I want to scream.

"But it's important for you to know that it's not too late for you to seek help," he says. "Even now..."

Then it hits me. *Shit.* "That's Grace's car. It's my cousin's car."

"Who?" asks Ryan oh so sweetly.

"You know who I mean." There's something stuck in my throat. It might be my heart. I don't know. But puking isn't out of the question. "What have you done to her?"

"You're forgetting again. I am incarcerated. There's no way I could have been involved."

Noah turns away from the window. "Sid, the police are here."

"Who is that?" asks Ryan, spitting out the words. "Who the fuck is that? You have someone there with you, you whore?"

I disconnect the call. His peace, love, and positivity sure didn't last for long. Hanging up on the asshole is a small victory, but one I will gladly take. And sure enough, someone knocks on the door. This spiraling sensation is a horribly familiar feeling. I take a deep breath and say, "Might be best if you move the board on the fence and get out the back way."

Noah pauses and stares at me for a minute. "Do you not want me here? Or do you think I don't want to be here?"

"I think this is quickly turning into a disaster that you don't need to be part of. Something's happened to Grace and…I don't want you getting caught up in this."

"Okay. I appreciate you trying to protect me. But unless you're asking me to leave, this has to be my choice."

I don't know what to say.

The knocking happens again. With more urgency this time.

Meanwhile, Noah takes a seat in one of Grandma's black leather and chrome armchairs. He pats his lap and Auggie jumps up to make himself at home. My eyes are watering suspiciously. But I will not cry in front of the cops. Not happening.

The coffee in my stomach has turned as sour as can be. What I need to know is if Grace is alive or dead. She invited herself into this situation for shitty reasons. But she sure as hell didn't deserve to get hurt or worse.

I blink repeatedly, stand up straight, and undo the hundred and one locks on my front door. No eye contact for the reporters standing out on the street. Keeping their distance due to a warning from the police officer, probably. My focus is all on the woman standing in front of me. She's about my size with white skin, long dark hair in a braid, and wearing a charcoal-colored suit. There's a very serious expression on her face. I wonder if it's what gave her identity away to Noah. She isn't someone I've met before. Which is not a bad thing.

"Sidney Walsh?" she asks.

"Yes."

"Detective Hahn." She holds up her badge and I.D. "I have a couple of questions I'd like to ask you."

Inviting a cop into my home is generally a no. But this isn't Officer Smith here to mess with me. And I would rather answer a couple of questions now on my own territory than be invited down to the station for something more serious. The other thing is…I need information now. She can tell me what the hell is happening.

I step back and she enters. The front door is immediately shut tight against the press. Detective Hahn gives a nod to my neighbor and the dog.

"What happened to Grace?" I ask. "Have you found a body?"

The detective gives me a long look before taking a seat on the couch. Her blank face is excellent. "Why don't we sit?"

There's no chance of me being still. I commence pacing back and forth in the small space. "I am guessing you don't have a body. Just the car. But there must have been signs of a struggle for you to be here, right? For this to be taken so seriously?"

Her chin rises just a little. I am taking it as confirmation.

"It's not even midday. So you found it what…early this

morning? The article online said it was left in the same national park as Briana Petersen."

"Where were you last night, Miss Walsh?" asks the detective.

"I was at a party next door until about ten and then here."

"Was anyone with you? Someone who could corroborate this?"

"Me," says Noah.

"And your name is?"

"Noah Allard. I'm her neighbor."

"You were together the entire time?" asks the detective, taking notes on her phone.

"Yes." I nod. "Apart from the five minutes it took me to walk home, unlock the door, and take my dog out back to pee."

"By then I was here," says Noah.

"Which I can confirm with footage from my security cameras. Though with them being mine you'd expect me to know how to get around them, right?"

"Why leave your own party?" she asks Noah.

"There were still some people there," he confirms. "I can give you names and contact details if needed. But I left because being with Sidney was more important."

She finishes typing. "Miss Walsh, how close are you to your cousin, Grace?"

"Please just tell me…is she…"

The detective stares at me. Then she sighs and says, "No body has been found. How close are you to your cousin?"

"And it was last night she went missing?"

"Yes," she answers in a terse voice. "Grace was seen leaving her motel room and getting into her car just after eleven. Now answer the question, please."

"You probably already know she arrived here a few days ago. Said it was to get out of town after breaking up with her fiancé. I think that part is true. That they broke up. But she wasn't so much here to see me as to get information and record conversations with me for the people making the podcast and documentary."

"The one called *Misled?*"

"Yes." I cross my arms over my breasts. Holding myself together seems appropriate. "Grace said she lost a lot of money from deposits for the wedding, and she was obviously desperate to haul her ass all the way up here. Vermont was somewhere she got sent as a kid. It wasn't somewhere she tended to visit for fun. Or at least, not as far as I am aware. But we hadn't seen or talked to each other since our grandmother's funeral eight years ago."

"You were unaware she was involved with the podcast?"

"I didn't have a clue. Found her creeping around at some stupid hour of the morning trying to…to find things to give them. Information on me or whatever."

"What did you do?"

"Told her to get out. That was the last time we talked."

The officer keeps typing. "There was no further contact via text or messaging or anything else?"

"No."

She just nods.

"Wonder if one of your people told the media about the connection to me?"

"That must have made you angry," she says, ignoring my snark. "Grace betraying you like that."

"We were close when we were kids. But like I said, it'd been a long time. And she did warn me she was broke."

"But still…"

I just shrug. It's not my job to help her make a case against me. I've probably said too much already. But she has to know she can rule me out as a suspect what with me having an alibi. Hooray for rediscovering sex on this particular night.

"If you weren't close, why did you let her stay?" asks the detective.

"Because she's family. I was feeling sentimental. It seemed like the right thing to do at the time."

Noah pats the dog and stays silent through all of this. His face is a careful blank. I don't know what he's thinking. Auggie on the other hand is busy licking a paw. He doesn't seem particularly bothered by the detective's presence. At least, he hasn't growled at her like he did the reporters.

"Have you listened to your cousin's segment on the podcast?" she asks.

"Yes."

"How did you feel about her insights into your life?"

"She barely knows me. I don't know if I would call her comments about me particularly insightful. Though I thought it was nice she pushed back on some of their bullshit."

"But not nice enough for you to reach out to her?"

"No," I say.

"Grace mentioned you have a tendency toward violence?"

"She mentioned I have a punching bag as part of a home gym. So do a lot of other people."

"Yes. But she also said she was scared of you. Did you ever threaten your cousin?"

"No."

"Then why was she afraid of you?"

"I don't know," I answer. "You'd have to ask her that."

"I hope I get the chance to."

"So do I."

The detective pauses. "Grace seemed to think you were searching for the bodies of other missing women. I'm surprised you'd want anything to do with that. Anything that would remind you of your ex. The memories of what happened can't be pleasant."

"They had to pry his hands from around my neck. So, no… not my favorite."

She waits for me to give her more. Then she says, "Any information you might have on the possible whereabouts of missing persons should be turned over to the police."

"In my experience, the police don't tend to listen to what I have to say. I tried to tell them ten years ago. How he would take me hiking. Some of the places where he liked to stop. They either wouldn't take me seriously, implying that I was a stupid girl who spread her legs for a monster and didn't know anything worth hearing. I'll spare you the actual slut-shaming language that was used. Or else they thought I was somehow involved and was misdirecting them to waste resources."

"This is about helping missing women, Miss Walsh. Not you processing your hurt feelings."

"You're right," I say. "It does hurt my feelings when your people harass me."

"That's a serious accusation."

"Easy enough to prove. Check out how many parking, speeding, and other types of fines have been issued to me in the last decade."

"Have you lodged any complaints about this supposed behavior?"

I don't bother to answer.

"I called your aunt earlier. She doesn't seem to be a fan of yours."

My mouth stays shut.

"She's driving up from New York now. Should be here by this evening," says the detective. "Is there anything you can tell me that might help with the investigation?"

I frown and think it over. "He's been in touch a couple of times lately. Ryan."

"It's highly unlikely he has anything do with this given he's still safely locked up." She frowns right back at me. "Is that unusual, him contacting you?"

"It'd been about a year since the last time he wrote. He's never tried to call me before. But he did this morning." I pause and think it over some more. Trusting the police is an issue for me. Obviously. "His girlfriend has also been hanging around."

Noah blinks but says nothing.

"You really think they could be involved somehow in your cousin's disappearance?" she asks, not bothering to hide the trace of disbelief.

There's a small possibility I sound paranoid. But such is life. "This has to be a copycat, right? Probably someone who's in contact with him. I know he's involved somehow. Why don't you look into those idiots who send him fan mail?"

The detective stands and gives me another of those long looks. Like she's trying to read my soul or something. She must come up empty since she says nothing.

"A state forest is a big area to search. When do you think they'll want volunteers?"

"I'd guess tomorrow morning," she says. "The crime scene and surrounding area will be processed today. Our people are out there looking. But there's rain forecast for this afternoon. Having dozens of people tramping through the woods and possibly disturbing any evidence won't matter so much after that."

I just nod.

"But you have to know, given the situation, your presence could well be more of a hindrance than a help." She heads for the front door. "Thank you for your time, Miss Walsh."

CHAPTER ELEVEN

SMALL RITUALS HELP ME NOT TO PANIC. BECAUSE LOSING my shit won't solve anything. Some of the coping mechanisms are things I learned in therapy. Taking deep even breaths as I redo the locks on the door. Setting my back against it and focusing on this safe space. Concentrating on the things I can control. The reporters are outside and can't get in— not if I don't let them. And any relevant information has been shared with the detective. There's nothing more I can do right now to help Grace and that absolutely sucks.

I can't wait to put in some time with my punching bag. To work out the anger and frustration. They might have a valid point about me and violence.

Noah is still sitting on the lounge chair. It's a special sort of magic how the sight of him calms me. Though it's the steady gaze that really gets me. Seems he has a settling effect on the dog too since the very good boy Auggie is asleep on his lap. Which is handy. We don't need him growling or barking at our unwanted visitors and making the situation any more stressful than it already is.

"Never been someone's alibi before," says Noah.

"Fun, huh?" I give him the weakest of smiles. Just truly pathetic.

"Tell me what you're thinking, Sid."

"She'll never have a chance to get her life together and figure out a new version of happy. It's why she said she came here. And I mean…obviously that wasn't all of it. But it felt like some of it was the truth."

He nods somberly.

"The similarities between her death and last time…leaving her car in the same park. Her hair being long. Maybe I am just being paranoid, but—"

"I highly doubt that."

"A woman going missing now in this way almost makes it look like Ryan either wasn't responsible, or at least not solely responsible, for what happened to Briana Petersen."

He thinks it over for a moment. "If I hadn't been here last night his bullshit story about you being the killer might have suddenly looked a whole lot more likely."

The man is absolutely right and I don't know what to do about that. But I settle for checking the messages in the group chat on my phone.

> Muriel: They're linking you to an abandoned car and missing woman. Call me.
>
> Me: Cop was just here. It's my cousin Grace.
>
> Muriel: Just saw that in an online chat. I am so sorry.
>
> Hana: Are you ok?
>
> Me: Yeah.

Hana: Security footage of her leaving her motel room and getting into her car last night has been leaked.

Me: Cop confirmed signs of a struggle at her car. Don't think they know much else.

Muriel: Should we come over?

Me: Reporters out front. Better not.

Hana: :(

"It isn't your fault," says Noah. "Whatever's happened to your cousin."

"I know. I just wish she'd gone back to New York. But if wishes were horses, beggars would ride. Grandma used to say that all the time. I didn't have a clue what she was talking about when I was little. Though I figured it had something to do with free ponies and I was down with that." Just watch me babble my heart out due to stress. Meanwhile my fingers are busy picking at the stitching in the hem of my tee.

Noah nods in understanding. "Ryan's new girlfriend has been hanging around?"

"It was her following us that night we walked to the lake. Did I tell you that?"

"No. When else have you seen her?"

"She followed me to the grocery store one day and gave me shit about stuff. Stood on the opposite side of the street another time and did some intense staring. And she was probably responsible for when you found the side gate unlocked. The day you were fixing the fence."

"You think she's been looking in your windows or something?"

I shrug. Because it's as good a guess as any. "My security cameras record over their data every twenty-four hours if you don't save it. She won't be on there. And it's not like it's illegal to go grocery shopping. So I have no real proof this is actually happening."

"And today's the first time you've talked to Ryan in all these years?"

"Yes. That letter you brought me the first time we met was from him. He likes to write me creepy notes now and then. Let me know he's got someone watching me and reporting back to him. He name-drops places I've been and comments on my hair and stuff."

A muscle pops in the side of his jaw. Big feelings are happening, but his voice remains calm. "He really lost his shit there at the end of the call."

"Yeah." There's not much I can say about it. "I didn't know I was involved last time. That I knew the killer and could possibly affect what was happening. But this time I know that I am somehow involved and it's still not helping."

"Baby, you can't affect anything." His use of the endearment makes my heart skip a beat despite this fucked-up situation. "You're not responsible for what's happening and none of this is under your control."

"I don't want to hear that."

"I know."

"There really is nothing I can do to help her," I say, my shoulders slumping.

"No. Not right now."

"Shit." There's every chance if I do any more deep breathing, my lungs will collapse. Just die from overuse or something. "You're still here. Are you sure you don't want to run screaming? No one would blame you."

"I'm good."

"Yes, you really are."

His shit-eating grin sure is something. "Now you're just trying to make me blush."

"I didn't mean it like that." I almost laugh. It's a close thing. "But I'm fine with you taking it that way."

He smiles and gently sets Auggie on the ground. The good dog heaves out an almighty sigh. So hard being him. Life ruined. Again. "We need to eat. Then what do you say we get out of here for a while?"

My head turns toward the lurking media outside. "Not sure if going out there is a good idea."

"Trust me," he says, holding out a hand. "I've got a plan."

It turns out the plan involves us moving the board and sneaking through the hole in the back fence. Through his house and into the garage where his motorcycle waits. He has a spare helmet for me to wear and it hides my face just fine. How the engine comes to life beneath me is a thrill. And molding myself against his back and wrapping my arms around his middle is even better. I want to hold on tight and never let go. He's officially made me a stage-ten clinger and doesn't even have the good sense to be worried.

Up goes the garage door and off we go. It's the same wondrous sense of freedom as standing on the lake shore beneath a sky full of stars. The world races past in a myriad of colors and nothing can touch us. We head north with the Green Mountains on one side and the Adirondacks on our other. The beauty of it all is breathtaking. A reminder of all the good things out there. This is exactly what I needed—him and this perfect moment.

And by the time we return, Grace's body has been found.

"My son has been a model prisoner. His therapist says he's made wonderful progress with the rehabilitation program and is earnest and engaged. He's accepted his culpability and made peace with the part he played in the tragic events that took place ten years ago." Ryan's mom stands tall and proud on the TV. A small crowd of people are gathered behind her holding candles. They're in one of the parks by the lake.

My cell sits on the coffee table. We decided a group call on speakerphone was the safest option. Though my small front yard is currently unoccupied care of what's happening on screen. The media have been lured away for the moment.

A cop car cruises past every hour or so. No idea if they're keeping an eye on me or what. It would be nice to think they're warning away any assholes wanting to try some vigilante shit. Abuse my already broken letterbox or something. But who knows what their agenda is.

Noah had things to do at his place. I doubt he'll leave me alone for long, however. As much as he likes to play it cool, he tends to worry.

"Making this speech at what was supposed to be a vigil for Grace is some bullshit," says Hana.

Muriel snorts. "Ballsy, bold, brazen. I can think of lots of b words that describe her."

"You can just say bitch. No one will mind." I chase two Advil with a mouthful of water. The headache from crying needs to go away. Tears don't help, but sometimes they happen. Such is life. And death, apparently.

"I object," says Hana. "I've met some banging bitches over the years. But this woman sure isn't one of them."

"I don't care what the police say," continues Dianne. "That the true perpetrator of these crimes is right now sitting at home in her living room is an outrage."

I raise my brows. "She's wrong about the crimes part. But right that I am in fact sitting in my living room."

"Her psychic probably told her you were," says Hana.

"We should ask for the lotto numbers."

"That woman should be rotting in a prison cell." Dianne all but trembles with emotion. "Not my sweet boy."

Muriel makes a noise. One indicating deep thoughts. "Notice she's not mentioning your name. Think she's worried you'll go after her for slander?"

"She has more money than me. You should see the house Ryan grew up in," I say. "Just getting legal advice last time cost a small fortune. Facing off with her and her team of lawyers doesn't seem particularly smart. But I also worry about giving her any more of a platform. Like publicly paying attention to her might legitimize her more in some way."

"It's complicated," agrees Hana.

Meanwhile, Dianne goes into detail about her darling homicidal son's most admirable qualities. How he played football in high school and volunteered for a local charity fundraiser. The way he would mow an elderly neighbor's yard when he was younger. And hasn't he been assisting with the prison literacy program for the last year?

My favorite stalker, Laura, stands beside her future mother-in-law with her hands clasped tight and a beatific smile on her face. She's just that sweet and sincere, apparently. The white sweater dress and silent stoic pose is a great aesthetic. This shit is probably going viral on social media. Seems my cousin's death is just adding fire to the #justiceforryan movement.

How low do you have to be to hijack a woman's death for your own agenda? Assholes.

"Smart of them to let her do the talking," I say. "Dianne has a background in local politics and knows how to spin."

Hana gasps. "Did you see that? Someone's wearing a Team Sidney t-shirt in the crowd!"

"Ha. They are so on my Christmas card list." My smile isn't big, but it's there. And its presence makes me feel like I am betraying Grace. I kind of want to throw something at the screen. But the only person that might hurt is me. And the TV of course. The way my emotions are all over the fucking place. I feel guilty and angry and a hundred other things. None of which are doing anyone any good. What we need to do is find out who killed my cousin. "They went to the trouble of either taking her to the same park or luring her out there where Briana Petersen was found. Why use a different method to murder her?"

"Strangling someone with your bare hands takes strength," answers Muriel. "The ability to subdue them and keep up the pressure. Brain death takes five or so minutes."

"A bullet to the back of the head is easier," says Hana. "They didn't ask you to identify the body?"

I shake my head. Not that they can see me. "No. I'm guess-ing my aunt had already arrived in town."

"Do you think you'll hear from her?" asks Muriel.

"I highly doubt it. She hated me before all of this. Her only child just got murdered, most likely because of a link to me. Those feelings will only be compounded now."

"Wonder if they tried to bury her out there," says Hana. "How closely did they follow what happened to Briana?"

"We need more information. The statement the cops made didn't tell us a damn thing."

There's a noise from the lock on the back door and in walks Noah. My heart does its usual belly flop at the sight of him. A tension inside me unwinds. I don't remember it being like this last time…so big and unwieldy and all consuming. It would make sense to slow down. Me and romantic relationships have an awful history, and he couldn't have chosen a worse time to get involved with me. Though his alibi sure saved my ass and then some. My mobile phone data would place me at home. But someone having actual eyes on you is better.

"Noah's back. Talk to you guys later." I pick up my cell and disconnect the call. Then I turn off the TV.

And here we are. Just him and me.

The thing is, blurting out I like him or love him or I don't know what is not a good idea. Not this soon. Not in the middle of all of this. However, there's this tangle of words sitting on my tongue just waiting to be set free. I'm not even sure what it is I want to say. A safer option might be performing an interpre-tive dance or reciting some bad poetry. Anything that doesn't involve throwing my panties and poor beat-up heart at the man.

His dark hair is damp and slicked back. And he's wearing

a fresh pair of jeans and a black tee. There are bruises beneath his eyes. A reminder of last night's lack of sleep. He's still the most beautiful thing I've ever seen.

"I tidied up the place and took a shower," he says matter-of-factly. "Tried to think of shit to do to give you some time to yourself. But then I got worried about you being on your own, so here I am."

"Hi."

"Hey." He tosses the key I'd given him yesterday in the air and catches it in his hand. "I think I'm going to hang on to this."

"Oh."

"Is that a problem?"

"No."

I've never given a significant other a key. The timing never seemed right with Ryan. Something which just might have saved my life. But the thought of Noah being a part of my world, of him able to come and go as he likes, is strangely pleasing. None of the everyday normal anxiety rears its ugly head at the idea.

"You'd tell me if he called again, right?" he asks.

"Ryan? Yes. Though I doubt he will. I'm really not that important to him. He just likes to mess with me now and then. Being in prison must get boring."

Noah makes a noncommittal sound. "What are you up to?"

"Guess I should try to get some work done." I wrinkle my nose. "I don't want to, but they sent over some files earlier for a rush job. The pressure is officially on."

He nods. Then he yawns. "I'm going to crash. Come get me if you need me. If you hear a noise outside you want investigated or you want some company or anything, okay?"

I give him two thumbs up. Like an idiot. Check out my smooth moves.

The edge of his mouth kicks up in amusement and he heads for the stairs. Noah is staying the night and sleeping in my bed. Again. This has not been a good day, but life doesn't entirely suck.

It's about two in the morning when he wanders outside. I'm lying on an old picnic blanket in the backyard. The perfect position for staring at the stars and thinking deep thoughts. Or nothing at all. With all of the trees standing guard along the fence line, you can almost believe you were out in the wild. Untouched by trouble and nowhere near civilization. Some nights it's a really calming idea.

He stretches out beside me with a sigh. "You okay?"

"Yeah. Just had a bad dream."

His voice is rough and low from sleep. "What was it?"

"The usual. Hands around my throat, and I can't breathe."

He frowns. A pair of jeans are all he wears. Lean muscle and messy hair are a delight in the moonlight. The cut of his jaw and the concern in his eyes. "Wake me next time."

"One of us should get us some sleep."

"Wake me next time," he repeats.

"Okay."

He grunts.

"The problem is the nightmare wakes me up, and then my brain gets busy thinking about things, and then I can't get back to sleep."

"What sort of things?"

"Anything really."

"You're an overthinker," he says.

"Like you wouldn't believe."

He looks me over, taking in the sleep shorts and tank. Then he rises on one elbow and checks out our surroundings. Auggie is asleep inside on his dog bed like a good boy. And the neighborhood is quiet as can be. All of the sensible sorts are fast asleep in their beds. Even the media are missing for now. Though knowing my luck they'll return tomorrow for more fuckery. This time of night is reserved for nocturnal creatures in this corner of the world.

Without a word, he hooks a couple of fingers in the side of my shorts and the panties beneath. Down my legs and off they go. Which is when he crawls between my legs. His face is positioned just so, and my legs are lifted over his thick shoulders. The heat of his body against the touch of the cooler night air is stirring in all sorts of interesting ways. Guess he enjoys al fresco dining, and who am I to complain?

He nuzzles my inner thigh. Rubs his mouth against my sensitive skin. The light graze of his stubble is a breathtaking thing. Just amazing. My nerve endings light up like fireworks. And everything low in my stomach seems hot and heavy. No part of me isn't focused on him and what he's doing. The feel of his breath against my sex is making me so wet. There isn't room in my mind for anything else. In this one moment, he's my whole world and I don't hate it. He traces the crease where my torso meets my leg with the tip of his nose. Just this ever so gentle touch is both too much and not enough. I need him a couple of inches over like my life depends on it. But of course, he takes his time.

Something I learned last night is how much he likes kissing. The man can make out for hours. And he kisses my labia now, sucking and licking with utmost skill. My eyes roll back in my head and the stars up high disappear. His thumbs hold my lips open as he lavishes me with attention. My heartbeat has moved south, sitting between my thighs. He fucks me with his tongue, eating me as if nothing else matters. As if he has never tasted anything better in his life.

The way this man goes straight to my head. Nothing could be more potent than having his mouth on me. My heels move restlessly against his back. My hands are tangled in his hair. No one has done this for me before. Not like this. Noah doesn't stop until I'm shaking from head to toe. He grips my thighs tight, holding me in place, as he lashes me with his tongue.

Someone's loudly panting and moaning and it's me. There's every chance I've even forgotten my own name. His talented tongue draws circles around my clit. Around and around until I lose my fucking mind. The teasing flicks of the tip of his tongue are killing me. I have unfortunately forgotten the English language. But someone needs to tell him to stop messing around and finish me off before I accidentally tear out his hair. Which is when the whole universe explodes. White light as far as the eye can see. Planets and stars and moons are reduced to ash and dust. It's like my body is gone, scattered to the corners of the earth by a strong breeze. The post-come float is heavenly. I never want to come down. But someone is putting my panties and shorts back on me before picking me up in strong arms.

"You'll sleep now," he says.

And he has me so relaxed he's probably right.

CHAPTER TWELVE

NOAH LEAVES FOR WORK AT NINE THE NEXT MORNING. Waking up next to him is everything. His arm thrown over my middle and his warm breath on the back of my neck. To sleep so soundly while sharing my space with someone is a revelation. The way we fit together seems perfect and simple so far. I don't want to get ahead of myself. I feel like cool girls live in the moment. They definitely don't indulge in a mental breakdown before breakfast. But death can do things to you. And the knowledge that Grace was murdered sits heavy in me like a stone.

I stumble down to the kitchen and make myself some coffee. Then I sit on the back steps beneath a clear blue sky while the very good boy performs a thorough inspection of the backyard. Auggie has settled in with no problems (give or take eating a pillow) and I love having him around.

A story on corruption amongst local cops has the media too busy to hang around my door. The sheriff's department is the shiny new dramatic headline on the local newspaper's site. The update on Grace's murder is sparse as can be. Nothing more than a rehash of previously reported facts with nothing new on offer. Though there is a photo of my aunt walking into the office of the Chief Medical Examiner. She seems so alone. I know logically there was nothing I could do to save my cousin. But the feelings of guilt linger just the same.

No idea what to do about it yet, however.

The desktop computer I do my work on is set up in the corner of the dining room on a nice old wooden desk. The study or war room is too full of the mission for me to be able to work in there. To be able to concentrate effectively. Certain areas of my life require compartmentalizing. Numbers were never really my thing. Odd how data inputting has become my main source of income. Guess life just happens like that sometimes.

The knock on my door comes at around midday. Auggie barks his little heart out. Just gives the noise his utmost commitment. I check the security camera on my cell and swear up a storm. Her presence here isn't a complete surprise. However, surely I can be forgiven for hoping this particular shitshow wouldn't happen.

"That's enough. Bed," I tell the very good boy. And he gives me a thoroughly disappointed expression but does as asked. It's with a heavy-ass heart that I unlock and open the door. "Hello, Aunt Beth."

She gives a sharp nod to the interior of the house, and I step back to let her enter. I don't love letting her into my safe space any more than I did the detective. But doing this on the doorstep isn't the answer. The woman used to intimidate the heck out of me when I was a child. Now, however, she seems smaller and a good deal less scary somehow.

I always knew she didn't like me. It wasn't something she particularly bothered to hide. Though to be fair, it's not like she behaved as if she liked anyone. The fights she and Grandma used to get into. She'd made the walls of the old house shake with her sharp words. Guess some people are just born bitter and angry.

Her hair is the same perfect shade of platinum blonde as I remember. And her features a sharper version of her daughter's. She wears her grief like armor. Though the black sheath dress she's wearing is creased as fuck. Something she never would have allowed under normal circumstances. My living room and life in general are given a derogatory sniff. But honestly, if that's the worst she does I'll count myself lucky.

"What was Grace doing here?" Her lips are a tight line. "It can't have been just to visit. She hadn't thought about you in years."

The comment is ouch though probably honest. "She was on a fishing expedition for the people making the documentary and podcast about me."

"Why was she involved with those cockroaches?"

"Guess she needed the money. She said she was broke."

Her brows draw down tightly. "What?"

"Apparently the deposits on stuff for the wedding and getting kicked out by her ex really set her back."

"Why didn't she tell me?" And she seems so honestly perplexed that her daughter didn't feel comfortable going to her during a time of trouble. "I would have helped her. But I hadn't heard from her in weeks."

My mouth opens and then closes. Because what the fuck can I even say? Telling a freshly bereaved mother that she's both horrific and terrifying is not the answer. Honesty is all well and good, but it's not going to help anyone right now.

She might even have figured the answer out for herself.

Because her chin trembles as she asks, "And how, Sidney, did my daughter end up dead?"

"I don't know."

Her hand lashes out and I see it coming. How the flat of her palm smacks hard into my cheek. The sting of her slap is a hell of a shock. She really gave the hit her all. I wonder if the woman plays pickleball or something. She has a great swing. And this assault, like her sniff of much disdain, is no surprise. Her pale pink–tipped dagger of a finger points at my face. "This is because of you, Sidney. You are the bad seed, the rotten fucking apple."

"I understand that you're hurting, Aunt Beth, but—"

"My useless sister was just the same. I told Mom to get rid of you, but did she listen? No. And you and your bullshit and your homicidal fucking boyfriend ended up getting her killed too!" The woman isn't saying anything I haven't heard before or even thought at times. Her words still hurt, however. She draws her arm back again, hand flat and ready to let fly at me again. This time when she goes to swing, however, I catch her wrist and keep it in a tight grip.

"No," I say in a firm voice. "I gave you the first one, but that's all you're getting."

She pulls her hand out of my hold. And I let her go.

"I am sorry your daughter is dead. But I don't know who killed Grace or why," I say and it's mostly the truth. Theories and guesses aren't going to give her any closure. "You should leave now, Aunt Beth. Go back to New York. There's nothing for you here."

"I couldn't agree with you more." The way her nostrils flare as she straightens her shoulders. "Don't come to her funeral. I don't want you there."

Noah: Further to previous conversations re our relationship, communication while separated is of utmost importance.

Me: Why are you texting at me like you're a lawyer?

Noah: I am now getting greens out of the walk-in fridge.

Noah: Thinking of working on a new sauce next.

Me: Okay.

Noah: I would kindly request that you take this seriously.

Me: My apologies for any perceived slight. I'm updating order codes for a customer. Which basically means I am sitting on my behind and inputting numbers while drinking my third coffee of the day.

Noah: What are you doing now?

Me: Still inputting numbers.

Me: How about you?

Noah: Still thinking about the sauce.

Me: This is amazing. I feel so close to you right now.

Noah: Yeah. I am usually right about things. Best for you to know that now.

Noah: How are you really doing?

Me: Honestly I am having a day. But you made
it better.

Noah: Tell me all about it later?

Me: You got it.

"Grace's body was found about half a mile from her car. She was killed by a single bullet to the back of the head," reports the podcaster.

The second dude says, "Such a shocking turn of events for all of us here at *Misled*."

"It certainly is, Steve, and our thoughts and prayers go out to her family and friends. While we have issued an invitation to Grace's mother, we have yet to hear back from her. But we hope to have her on the podcast real soon."

I snort. "I highly doubt that."

Hana, Muriel, and I are seated on cushions around the coffee table. Some nights are sitting-on-the-floor-and-eating-your-feelings sort of occasions. We ordered palak paneer, chicken saag, shrimp biryani, cheese naan, rice, and raita. Auggie sits beside me watching every bite of food like his life depends on it. As if he's starving and hasn't been fed in forever. The drama is real.

I haven't told my friends about the visit from Aunt Beth. There's no mark on my face and honestly, I would rather forget it ever happened. I will, however, tell Noah due to his honesty-is-best policy.

"So, who do you think did it?" asks Steve. "Because you know who my money's on."

Hana shakes her head. "This pair of dicks."

"For our new listeners, Grace was in Vermont to talk to her

cousin Sidney Walsh for us. I trust you're all familiar with that name." And the fucker actually chortles. "I think we're about to see sales of the Team Ryan merchandise go through the roof."

I wipe my hands with a napkin. "Another woman has died and they're talking about t-shirts."

"There are respectful, ethical true crime investigators out there," says Muriel. "Why they gave these two craven assholes the opportunity to make a documentary and expand their plat-form, I will never understand."

"Grace's bravery in facing down her cousin and joining our fight for truth and justice ending in this horrific way has been a heavy blow to everyone here at *Misled*. We were hoping she might have more information or been able to offer more in-sight into Sidney's supposed project to find the bodies of other women who went missing ten years ago during what there is reason to believe was her original reign of terror," says Steve. "Of course, searching for bodies that she may well have buried in the first place is either some sort of delusion or diversion on her part. Is it just a ruse so she has an excuse to keep visiting the graves she dug herself and reliving the thrill of killing those women?"

"You're absolutely right, Steve. Tell us in the comments if you think Sidney killed her cousin. And remember to hit that subscribe button while you're here, folks! You're going to want to stay up to date on this thrilling investigation. Speaking of which, we've also had some exciting news from Ryan's legal team today," continues the other podcaster. "They had what they're describing as a promising meeting today with the local D.A.'s office. There's not much they can say just yet. However, efforts to have Ryan retried are full steam ahead!"

"Dianne must be so relieved."

"She is indeed. I talked to Ryan's mom earlier and she wanted us to thank everyone who's signed the petition and been helping by putting pressure on the local authorities."

"Thank goodness they didn't let the sad news about Grace's death slow their roll." Hana takes a sip of wine. "That would have been such a downer."

"Onwards and upwards," I say with much sarcasm.

Auggie's ears suddenly twitch as he leaps to his feet. All thoughts of me and my meal are forgotten, apparently. He turns to face the front door and starts barking.

Muriel clutches at her chest. "Goodness gracious."

"Where are you, Sidney?" a voice yells from the street. "Get out here, you bitch."

I hit pause on the podcast and get to my feet. "Is Mars in retrograde or something?"

A quick check of my cell confirms the identity of the idiot. The one who has now fallen over and is sitting in the gutter with a beer in one hand and his head in the other. Grandma was a big believer in karma. She always said it was wrong to enjoy the trials and misfortunes of others. Therefore, I really hope she's not watching me from heaven, or the afterlife, or wherever. That would be so awkward right now.

"Good boy," I say to Auggie, giving him a pat to calm him down.

"Should I call the cops?" asks Hana.

"He *is* the cops."

"Shit."

"That means there's an even greater chance he might have a gun on him," says Muriel wisely.

Mrs. Lawson from next door appears and proceeds to tear the man apart with her bare hands. Or her harsh words, as the case may be. Officer Smith doesn't pull a gun on my neighbor, thankfully. And given all the years he's been harassing me, this is an opportunity too good to miss. No matter how foolish it might be, I am overdue a win. Even one this small and deeply petty and stupid.

With my trusty baseball bat waiting behind the door, I perform the unlocking ritual and open the house to the cool night air. I make sure to stay on my front porch. There's no need for me to go near him.

"She got me suspended," says the man with snot running down his face. "Without pay."

Christmas seems to have come early. My smile is more than a little malicious. "No. It was your own behavior that did that, Officer Smith. And I only spoke to the detective yesterday. The investigation into you and your shenanigans has probably been going on for a while now, hasn't it?"

"You don't know shit." Bullies sure don't like being called out on their nonsense. Not one bit. But he's done more than just hassling me when Noah and I were walking back from the lake that night. The bulk of the speeding, parking, and other types of fines I received over the years were written by this man. "I was protecting the community!"

"No you weren't."

"Yes I was!"

"No you…okay. I am actually going to stop now while we can still tell the difference between the drunken idiot and me."

Hana snorts. "Good idea."

But Mrs. Lawson crosses her arms. So much disapproval

of the inebriated asshole. This might well be the only time she and I have agreed on anything. "Pull yourself together and get out of here before I feel the need to phone your friends on the force and ask them to remove you," she tells the man.

He gives her the stink eye. But he does indeed haul himself to his feet. "You'll get yours, Walsh."

"Did you really just threaten me in front of three witnesses?" I ask. "Seriously?"

He grunts and snarls and whatever. But he's out of drunken bravado. His progress down the shadow-lined street is as haphazard as can be. I honestly wouldn't be surprised if he crashed in someone's yard and woke up tomorrow to a sprinkler in the face.

Mrs. Lawson gives me a long look before turning to head home without another word. It might just be my imagination, but her usual level of distrust and ire seems to be missing. Which is interesting.

"Get that out of your system?" asks Muriel drily.

"I think so," I say with a smile. Which is when it occurs to me. "Oh shit, who's guarding the food from the dog?"

And sure enough, the little dude is busy licking my plate clean. The doggy smile he gives me is huge. "Auggie. For shame."

"What a good dog only eating Sidney's food," says Hana, giving him a pat. "You're such a good dog, aren't you?"

Muriel wanders back out of the kitchen with a fresh plate in hand. "Lucky there's leftovers."

"Thank you." I sit down and Auggie curls up next to me with a contented happy sigh. As he should with a full stomach. "So our list of suspects for Grace's murder is basically everyone."

"Guns are one of the weapons of choice when it comes to killing your girlfriend," says Hana. "What are the chances her ex followed her up here?"

I sigh. "I don't know. All she really said about him was that he was a judgmental asshole. But that might have been more about her trying to make me think she was on my side, so I'd talk to her about all this stuff."

"You don't think it's more likely that her death had something to do with Ryan?" asks Muriel.

"Just trying to keep an open mind at this stage," says Hana. "But her link to Sidney, that she was in town for the podcast, and her being found in the park are all curious as fuck. Could be a copycat killer. Someone trying to compete with Ryan or maybe someone who wants his attention."

"Could definitely be," I agree.

"Or it might be someone trying to mess with you."

My eyes open painfully wide. "They're doing great so far. Consider me messed with."

"We need more information," says Muriel, her brows pinched tight together. "How do we get it?"

I tear off a piece of naan. Thinking requires carbs and lots of them. "She was in town for the money. It would be great to get a look at her bank accounts. But in lieu of that, I'm going to try the motel where she was staying and see if anyone will talk to me. I mean…we were family. They might tell me something useful."

"It's worth a try," says Hana.

Muriel nods. "I agree. But should you really be going on your own?"

"Alone is less intimidating and it's a public place." I shrug. "Should be fine. It's been a while since I've seen my stalker in the flesh. She's probably too busy with other stuff right now to bother hassling me. We have no actual evidence anyone else means me harm."

"Just your cousin's dead body," says Muriel drily. And yeah, she's got a point.

CHAPTER THIRTEEN

RACE WAS STAYING AT A HOTEL OUT BY THE HIGHWAY. A nice three-star sort of place. No idea if she chose it or the podcast put her up there. I head out around sunset the next day since work took longer than expected due to a new account. This might be a total waste of time. But I have to do something. I can't just sit around any longer waiting for news.

The hotel is a big old four-story brick building. While the lighting in the parking lot could be better, the place is packed, so I wind up parking on a grassy area in the back. Some of the trees surrounding the lot have started to change color. Green giving way to red, orange, and gold. Guess summer is officially over for another year. A dark sedan seemed to follow me some of the way, but they didn't turn off into the hotel parking lot with me. Not that I have any idea what car Laura drives. But there's been no sign of my stalker for a while now. Which is curious. Perhaps the push to have Ryan retried is taking up her time. Or did shadowing me just stop being fun?

Inside, the air is cool and stale. Signs in the foyer advertise a Hemp and Cannabis Conference happening. A folk band plays in the bar area to a good-sized audience. One that is as mellow as can be. And the person at reception looks bored as can be. They're around twenty. Curvy, with white skin, an assortment of piercings, and a gaze that's glued to the computer screen.

I approach the desk with a wide hopeful smile. "Hi."

"Hello." The tag on their neat and tidy shirt says their name is Harper. "How can I help you?"

"My cousin stayed here a couple of days ago. She's the woman who went missing and was found out at the park." Notice the way in which I delicately omit the word "murder." As if not using it will change anything. "I was wondering if—"

"We can't talk about that," they say flatly.

Of course I'm not the first person sniffing around for information. No doubt the media and an assortment of amateur detectives have already been by. So this is when I somehow endear myself to them. This part of the process is usually left to Muriel or Hana. They both have better people skills. Less of a *warning: possible psycho killer* attached to their name and/or face.

But Harper raises their gaze from the screen and stops cold at the sight of me. "Oh. It's you. Sidney, right?"

"Yeah. Hi."

They stare at me for a moment. Then their gaze flits around the room before settling on me once more. Checking no one is nearby or listening into our conversation. Like the band's rousing rendition of "Jolene" would allow for such a thing.

"She came down here to complain about the towels," says Harper, leaning in and lowering their voice. "It was about this time of night. I don't know what she expected me to do about it. They're okay quality, but this isn't the Hilton."

I just nod.

"Her phone rang, and she answered it on speaker. The

woman on the phone was pissed off. Told her to take her off speaker. Then your cousin said, 'Why are you calling me? I did what you wanted.'"

"Huh."

"That's all I can tell you. It's the same thing I told the police."

"Was she young or old, do you think? The person who called her?"

"Not a clue. There was a band playing that night too. I couldn't hear well enough to tell you anything more. But your cousin, she wasn't happy. I mean, she was already upset about the towels. Then hearing from this person made her mouth do the puckered thing. You know what I mean?"

"I know what you mean."

"The cops still have her room sealed and some of her stuff in there. But I can't show it to you, sorry."

"I don't want to get you into any trouble. Thank you for talking to me."

"Sure. For what it's worth, I don't think you killed those women," says Harper. "I've watched a ton of reels about it and honestly I just don't get that vibe from you."

"Thanks."

They just nod. "You're welcome."

"I think you can do anything you set your mind to," says Noah later that night. "Is that the correct supportive response?"

"Not a clue. I've never actually figured out what I'm supposed to say. I mean, I guess it's good that I don't look like a homicidal maniac. But anyone could probably kill given the right circumstances, right?"

"I am going to go with noncommittal on this one. It'll help me sleep better at night."

"Fair enough."

He gives me an amused glance as we wander down the street, away from home. Amusing this man just might be my new favorite thing. Being someone who brings a smile to his face.

Both Auggie and I needed a walk. To be out in the fresh night air brings a welcome reprieve. Clouds cover most of the sky, with stars peeking through here and there. And a cool breeze is blowing in from the north. We're heading into sweater weather. Noah didn't like the idea of us going on our own, and I love being in his company, so this is a win all round. He holds both the leash and my hand.

"Probably a good thing you don't have murdery vibes," he says eventually.

"I think so. What's a murdery vibe anyway?"

"What did you find out at the hotel?"

"Not much," I say. "An angry woman called her on the phone. Grace answered, 'What do you want? I've already done what you asked.'"

He frowns.

"It doesn't sound related to the cancelled wedding. She said something about the podcasters not being the only ones willing to pay right before I threw her out. But I don't know who she meant. Some other media outlets maybe?"

"Hmm."

"Like I said, it's not much to work with. My aunt said she hadn't talked to her in weeks, so it definitely wasn't her."

His frown intensifies. "Still can't believe she hit you."

"Yeah. That was something." I chew on my bottom lip. "I

wonder if the police have Grace's cell. Nothing's been said about it in the media. Though the person calling her could have used a burner or something. Who knows."

"You're assuming the call had something to do with her death?"

"It's all we've got to go on right now." I shrug. "Grace doesn't seem like the type to agree to clandestine meetings in national parks in the middle of the night. But if they lured her out there with the promise of money…"

A line appears between his dark brows. "You think the podcast people were involved?"

"No. I don't think they killed her. They are, however, the reason why she was here."

"It would be a pretty extreme way to get publicity."

"Yeah. They were right about there being a proven history of people inserting themselves into investigations. I have a theory about it being a copycat. Someone who wants my ex's attention," I say. "What if the killer couldn't get close to the cops, but could get in with the podcasters? It's the next best thing. They have access to Ryan and he's like a rock star to some of them."

"That's so messed up."

I nod and think it over. "Maybe I should give the detective a call and ask for an update. I doubt she'll tell me anything, but it's worth a try. The idea that whoever did this is just walking around out there…"

He gives my hand a squeeze. "They caught your ex. I am sure they'll catch this person too."

"I hope so. The best use of my time is still probably focusing on where Ryan buried the other women's bodies. It's our best chance of keeping him behind bars."

Auggie steers us off the road and toward a tree. There's peeing and sniffing to be done.

"What are you going to do when all of this stops dominating your life?" asks Noah.

"That'll be a beautiful day. I don't know."

"Something worth thinking about."

"Move to another town where I am not so well known maybe," I say. "But I love it here. I'm not sure I could stay away forever."

"Hmm."

"You know what I haven't done in a long time?" I turn to him with a small smile. "Gone on a vacation."

"Now there's something we could be planning. Are you thinking sun and sand or what?"

"A beach would be good. Somewhere with a totally different vibe."

"How about Havana?" he asks. "We could spend a week soaking up the sun and eating Cuban food. Or if you want to go further afield, there's Thailand. The street food there is supposed to be amazing."

"I don't even have a passport."

"We need to get you a passport."

Auggie takes a keen interest in the remains of some asters. It won't be long before the last of the late summer flowers die off and fall takes over. Then all of these gardens will start giving way to stick season, followed by the white of winter. Seasons keep rolling along year in and year out. In a way, it's comforting how life just keeps keeping on. We're only a couple of blocks away from the waterfront now. Walking down quiet streets with most of the houses sitting in darkness.

"You haven't told me how things are at work with Jade," I say with a wince.

And he winces right back. "We're both keeping it professional."

"Okay."

"No one is universally loved, Sid."

"I know. We're all the villain in someone's story, right?"

He grunts.

Which is when I see the vehicle. A dark sedan with tinted windows rolling slowly down the street, right behind us. And it's not like we're strolling in the middle of the road. We're walking on the grass so the dog can inspect people's front yards. There's plenty of room for the driver to go around us and get on with their night, if that was what they wanted. But it isn't what they do. Nope. They continue trailing us.

Auggie tugs on the leash, leading Noah toward a garden gnome posed beside a mossy boulder in someone's yard. It's a smiling statue wearing a hat at a jaunty angle. No idea what the thing could have possibly done to upset him, but my dog lifts his leg and pees like his life depends on it. Noah raises his brows at me and waits patiently for the canine to be done. Which is apparently going to take an eternity.

And the car is still hanging behind us, moving slowly in and out of the pools of light cast by the streetlights. The driver's-side window lowers. What are the chances this is the same sedan from earlier, when I drove out to the hotel?

There's something awfully familiar about this, and I have the worst feeling in the pit of my stomach. All of the dread. "Noah..."

"Yeah?" He turns my way again. Then he sees the car coming closer at such a sedate pace and frowns. "What the hell?"

I half expect a hand with a gun to appear out the side window. But no. Tires suddenly scream and the scent of burnt rubber fills the air. The car lurches forward, veering off the road, right toward me. I turn and sprint down the street. Leading them away from Noah and Auggie. Thank fuck I wore tennis shoes. Auggie starts barking and Noah shouts something. My heart is hammering, blood pounding loudly behind my ears. But it's not enough to drown out the roar of the oncoming engine.

I have a head start, but it's only going to take them a couple of seconds to catch up to me. I know that any moment now the car is going to hit me. Squish me like a bug, or send me flying into outer space. Turning toward a house might be my best move. I have all of a moment to make up my mind.

The next streetlight is a while away, but in the yard ahead of me is a big old tree. It's not a good plan, but it's all I've got. I sprint straight for the tree. To hide behind it or something. The muscles in my legs start to burn. You need to be a special kind of person to commit vehicular homicide. To want to crash your car into someone. And I hope they're just that fixated on me.

There's a pickup truck parked in front of the yard, leaving no room for the driver to make a last-minute change in direction. If they follow me, they're fucked. But what I didn't account for is the tangle of gnarled roots at the tree's base. The toe of my shoe catches and my own momentum sends me sprawling on the cold hard ground.

It's deafening…the crash when the car hits the tree. Metal screeches and sparks fly as the bumper bar wraps around the trunk and the front of the car compresses. And the mighty old tree groans but miraculously doesn't give. I am lying there waiting to be dead or something. I don't know. The car is so close to me. But it doesn't happen.

Auggie's warm wet tongue drags up the side of my face. I have never been so grateful to get covered in doggie slobber. Best worst sensation ever.

"Sid," says Noah, eyes wide with panic. "Are you okay?"

"Hey."

He carefully helps me up to my feet. I am dazed and confused, shaking from head to toe. Like you do after a damn near-death experience. I think I am in shock. But apart from some bruises from hitting the ground, and small cuts from broken glass, I seem to be mostly unharmed. Which is fucking amazing and definitely not the case for the person inside the vehicle.

The woman is like a broken doll propped up in the driver's seat. Her usually perfect hair and makeup are all messed up. Blood seeps from her nose and the corner of her mouth. Given the force she hit the tree with, the front half of the car seems partially embedded in her chest.

"Hi, Dianne." I watch her through the window. "I honestly expected you to be Laura. But I should have known."

Noah is already dialing emergency services.

Dianne spits out blood and sneers. She's deep in her villain era. At least now we know her son came by his homicidal tendencies honestly. "Your cousin was mouthy too."

"That was you, huh?"

She tries to laugh but she's fading fast. The way blood is bubbling on her lips isn't a good sign. And I just stand there and watch like I bought a ticket for the whole damn gruesome show.

"H-he's going to get out," she says, struggling to speak.

"I highly doubt it now. You messed up making it look like I killed Grace. I have an alibi for that night. But I'm guessing you already know that. It's what made you desperate enough to do this shit."

It takes her a moment to force out the words. "The police want to talk to me but…I won't…give them the satisfaction."

"Getting away with murder is harder than it looks. Your son could have told you that."

Her head slumps to the side as her gaze dims. No idea if she's actually dead, or unconscious. Nor do I really care. Some people are devoid of humanity. Dianne deserves this dismal ending and the mess she made. And if this thought makes me an unkind or heartless and harsh person, then so be it. I will be out here representing the bitter bitches. Because the truth is, I am not big on forgiveness when it's neither asked for nor earned.

Auggie sits at my feet, pressing his small warm body against the side of my leg. Being a comforting presence. Lights have turned on in nearby houses. Sleepy and stunned locals start to gather on the road and grass around us. Some of them are even holding up phones to record the scene. And soon enough, sirens can be heard racing our way. Noah carefully wraps me in his arms and I hold onto him for dear life.

The last time I was being assessed in the back of an ambulance, my ex had tried to kill me. It sucks to be in a similar situation. Due to a member of the same family even.

Imagine living a quiet life. What would that even look like? To not have two members of the same family try and send you to the other side. How wild. Noah is nearby giving a statement while Auggie lounges at his feet. I get sort of frantic if they're out of sight. Like I keep needing to know they're okay.

I had never seen a dead body before. Never watched someone dying. And the experience has made me no closer to understanding the kick her son gets out of it. Though he got off on the cruelty and control. On being the one responsible for taking that life.

The paramedic shines a light in my pupils and tells me to follow their finger. One of those silver blanket things is wrapped around me, though the shaking stopped a while back. I think I was in shock. Now, I'm just tired after the adrenaline crash. I mean, my skinned elbow stings, but that's hardly something to bother bitching about.

The paramedic smiles and says, "You'll live. Take it easy for a day or two. Just to be careful."

"Thanks."

Detective Hahn approaches with a very serious face. She is not happy to be out here in the middle of the night. Fair enough.

"She said she killed Grace," I say. "Basically."

She turns to frown at the small crowd gathered behind the police lines. An assortment of reporters and camera operators along with locals and the plain curious. "I've been looking for her to discuss some phone calls and payments made to your cousin."

"So she was taking money from Dianne too?" I think it over. "Grace was probably supposed to make me look worse than she did. I think that's what the angry phone call was about that night at the hotel. The reason Dianne gave her for wanting to meet."

"Maybe," says the detective. "I am just grateful we can hopefully give your aunt some closure."

"Yeah."

She pulls out her cell to record our conversation. Starting by giving the date and time. "Give me the rundown on what happened, Sidney. What were you doing out here?"

"We were walking the dog. Going to the lake and back again," I say. "Then I noticed the same car that followed me earlier when I went to the hotel where my cousin was staying was following us now."

"Why did you go there?"

"To see the place and ask some questions."

Her expression isn't happy. "And it was definitely the same vehicle?"

"I believe so."

"Have you seen it before today?"

"It might have been parked on our street the other night. When Grace went missing. But I don't know for sure."

"You told me Ryan's girlfriend had been hanging around," she says.

"She has been. Though I haven't seen her for a while. But apparently Dianne decided to get in on the action too." I set aside the lightweight silver blanket. "Auggie, my dog, was peeing on the gnome a couple of houses back. Noah was holding the leash. I noticed the car just hanging behind us and then it started coming toward me. No chance I could outrun it, so I headed for the tree instead."

"You were lucky."

"Very. She said Grace was mouthy. That Ryan was going to get out. Then she mentioned you wanted to talk to her and she didn't want to give you the satisfaction."

"Was that everything she said?"

"I think so." I take a deep breath. Then I take another. "Grace died because of me. I knew that was the likelihood… but it sucks to know for sure."

"How did you contribute to what happened to your cousin? What deliberate steps did you take that you were cognizant of that were likely to result in her demise?"

I frown.

"That's what I thought. You didn't." She presses stop on her cell and gives me a look. "Do you really think you have a chance of finding those other missing women's bodies?"

"I don't know. I hope so. But with any luck, this will slow down the #justiceforryan movement. Cast some doubt on his supposed innocence. Give us more time to search. He needs to stay behind bars for everyone's safety."

"Keep in touch, Miss Walsh," she says.

Noah wanders over with Auggie in his arms. "He's decided he's had enough. We've been offered a ride home by an officer. Want to go?"

"That sounds like a great idea."

"How did it go with the detective?"

"I sense that she thinks I'm a drama queen."

His brows rise. "Someone just tried to run you over. I feel like you're entitled to a moment or two."

"Mm."

Detective Hahn talks to another officer near the car wreck. Screens are being erected to shield the site from both the media and the general public—to stop them from getting a gory picture. Who knows how long it will take to remove the body from all the twisted metal. There's a sea of lights from cameras behind the police lines. No doubt some of those news crews are filming us right now.

Noah leans in and places a kiss on my forehead. While Auggie takes the opportunity to lick me on the chin. Such a very good boy. One day my life will be normal. Not today, obviously. But one day.

"Wish I knew what I'd done to deserve you two," I say. "Because guaranteed I would do a whole lot more of it."

Noah smiles. And that smile almost makes getting flattened like a pancake seem worthwhile. Almost.

CHAPTER FOURTEEN

AURA CRIES IN SUCH AN AESTHETICALLY PLEASING fashion. It's sort of disturbing how good she is at it. Over the next couple of days, I watch her on the news and various other shows. The woman has turned her prospective mother-in-law's attempted homicide and head-on collision with a tree into both a very sad thing and a publicity boon for the #justiceforryan movement.

"The immense sadness and pressure that Dianne was under these past ten years…that dear sweet woman was tormented by what happened to her son." Insert a tear rolling over the smooth curve of Laura's cheek here. "How his life was derailed by this one dreadful relationship. Is it any wonder she snapped and acted so out of character?"

You would think the whole trying-to-run-me-down thing was an unfortunate mishap, or accident, according to this woman. Her sweetness and sincerity along with the vaguely trad wife vibes she's giving off are working wonders for the cause. Since neither Noah nor I release a statement, Laura's spin on things gets good airtime. Though thankfully some people are pushing back and questioning her narrative.

The official ruling on what occurred will take time. But Dianne's actions over the last few days and the tire marks on the road tell a definite story. Her intentions are clear, for those willing to see. But burying the truth and confusing the situation is how her son got away with the lesser charge of manslaughter. It's how he's hoping to have the charge dropped to accessory with time served. No wonder they're trying to pull the same trick again now. Dianne might be beyond caring about her reputation. However, it still matters to Ryan and Laura. They're all about the thoughts, prayers, and monetary donations to help cover his ongoing legal costs.

Some news crews stood in front of my house on the day after the crash. But they eventually got bored and went away. My policy of not feeding the media beast is helping to protect our privacy. Sort of. I can't actually stop them from hanging around and attempting to get a soundbite out of me. Auggie gave them a good barking at before turning his back on them and going to sleep. Such is his disdain for the press.

Meanwhile, Mateo gave me a high-five for not getting hit by a vehicle. He even took it easy on me since we were working out the night after the crash. I didn't have to do a ridiculous amount of pushups for once. We still did some sparring, however. Sore muscles and gross scabby elbows will only get you so far.

On the second night after the crash, I decide to cook for Noah. Normalcy is needed. Though I also want to show him I am not completely useless in the kitchen following the French toast debacle. My grandmother would doubtless haunt me if I didn't make the man her favorites—regional dishes she served me from a young age. These include a boiled dinner, which is corned beef cooked with garlic, peppercorns, a bay leaf, cabbage, and a variety of root vegetables served with mustard. And a homemade apple pie with a chunk of cheddar cheese.

"I'm not sure about this," he says, inspecting the slab of cheese. "Don't get me wrong…apple and cheese are great together. But I feel like accompanying apple pie is more of a sweet sort of situation."

"Welcome to Vermont."

"You're not going to serve me sugar on snow?"

"Grandma was old school when it comes to sugar on snow. She didn't agree with using shaved ice. So we have to wait for the right time of year for that one."

"I respect her wishes."

"Thank you. That means a lot to me."

The corner of his mouth edges up some. "Okay. Let's do this."

We're seated at the dining table. Which I actually managed to clear of bills, books, and other assorted shit like an adult. Candles are burning and music is playing. There's a vague air of romance to the scene. We're even using Grandma's vintage stoneware dishes and her heavy-ass wineglasses. The ones I used with Grace. It's a bittersweet memory.

Dinner started at ten thirty since that was when he got back from work. What time of the night or day it is doesn't bother me. So long as we're spending time together. Much more of this and I'll be drawing hearts around our initials in my notebooks. The truth is I don't know how to handle being this happy. But I like it a lot.

Noah spends the night here every night. He's done so since we got together, and is showing no signs of stopping. His clothes are on my bedroom floor, and he has his own toothbrush in the bathroom. We have officially entered a state of domestic bliss. A place where I would love to linger for a good long time.

"Muriel has invited you to bingo, by the way," I say as he chews and pulls thoughtful faces. Noah takes his tasting duties seriously.

"I've never been to bingo. This is interesting. Excellent pie crust."

"Glad you approve. Do you want ice cream now?"

"Yes, please."

I smile and steal the ungrateful man's piece of cheddar on the way to the freezer. One of us knows how to properly appreciate cheese.

Police lights are hard to miss, so I notice them right away as a cruiser is pulling in front of my house. No siren is blaring. But the lights are enough to stop me dead in my tracks. "No."

"What's wrong?" Noah is already up, out of his chair, and looking where I'm looking. It doesn't take Auggie long to stir from his dog bed in the living room and do some barking. "Good boy. Settle down."

I have the front door open before they manage to knock. Two officers in uniform are standing on the front porch at eleven o'clock at night. My heart goes into apoplexy at the sight. Because there's no way they have good news.

A Black woman with short natural hair asks, "Sidney Walsh?"

"That's right."

"I am Sergeant Mayhew, and this is Corporal Yang."

"What happened?" I ask, my shaking hands curled tight into fists. "Has another woman died?"

"No. No one is dead. But Ryan Brody has escaped from prison."

It doesn't take long for the news to get around. To those still awake at least. The hunt for Ryan is being broadcast all over the place. Reporters are filming updates standing outside the prison fences. Photos of Ryan and a missing guard at the jail by the name of Maggie Young are being shared far and wide. In her work uniform, she appears to be a calm and competent woman with long blonde hair. Just his type. The plea from her husband asking for her to be returned unharmed is heartbreaking. But it seems far more likely the woman knew exactly what she was doing, and was a willing participant. Rumors are rife that Ryan wooed her. It wouldn't be the first time he charmed someone into something.

Social media is full of theories about where he is and what he's going to do next. The option of lopping off my head is winning one poll by over a thousand votes. People are wild. I'm not sure how much more of this I can handle. And throwing my cell into Lake Champlain is not out of the question.

"So he either ran out of patience or thought his mom being exposed as a murderer was going to hurt his chances of getting the charges reduced to time served," I say to the detective.

"Perhaps," says Detective Hahn over the speaker. She calls not long after the two officers arrive. "We'll be guarding your house for the time being. Just to be careful."

"They're saying he romanced a jail guard and they're on the run together?" I ask.

"We believe that to be correct," answers the detective.

"There are extensive phone records between him and a corrections officer."

"Charming psychopath strikes again," I say. "Let me guess… she used a burner phone to hide what was happening?"

"What we do know for certain is that he left the prison grounds at around one in the afternoon. The reason given was he was attending a supposed court appointment. But he and the guard never arrived at the courthouse," she says. "Miss Walsh, where do you think he would go?"

"I've hardly talked to him in ten years. How would I know?"

"His girlfriend Laura is currently unable to be located, and his cellmate isn't talking. You're all I've got to work with right now. Would he stay in the local area?"

"He could cover a lot of ground in ten hours."

"Yes, he could. The official vehicle used for the escape was found at a train station in Essex Junction. And the guard's personal vehicle has been located parked outside some shops in Milton."

"Fast work. But the guard…has her body been found?"

"No. We believe they're still together. For now."

"Milton is north of us. If they left the car there, he probably wants you to think they're heading in that direction. Going to Canada to get lost out in the wilderness or something."

"Hmm."

"It's not like he used to talk about backup plans with me. Just in case he got caught. I had no idea he was a homicidal maniac, remember?"

"Can you think of any reason he might stay in town?" she asks.

"I get that you think I'm a lure for him. That's why there are cops sitting outside my house. But I'm just not convinced."

Nothing from the detective.

I think it through. And none of my thoughts are nice. "He wrote once to tell me how pretty I was the night he got captured. How soft my skin was and how wide my eyes were."

"He meant while he was strangling you?" asks the detective.

"Yeah."

Noah shifts in his chair. The muscles in his jawline are taut.

"I think he was encouraging Laura to stalk me," I say. "From some things she said. Being free would take precedence over messing with me for most people. But with the way his mind works, I just don't know."

"Would he blame you for his mother's death?"

I frown in thought. "He was good at handling Dianne. Playing the part of the loving son to get what he wanted. But the stuff he would say to me about her sometimes when she wasn't around…I don't really know how much he cared about her. What mattered the most to him was his ego and maintaining control of situations."

Detective Hahn sighs. "Keep your doors locked, Miss Walsh."

The call ends and I set my cell on the table. Noah is still sitting where he has been the whole time. On the plate in front of him is the forgotten slice of apple pie. And the pint of ice cream is nearby sitting in a small pool of water. So much for our romantic dinner.

"We could go," he says. "Hit the road and get out of here. Go find that beach we were talking about."

"Leave the restaurant without a head chef?"

"They could handle things for a while." He cocks his head. "How about we drive cross country. Take you and your dog to meet the Pacific Ocean?"

My brows are as high as can be. "You want to drive across the country with me?"

"Whatever it takes to keep you safe and get you the hell away from him."

My smile is small but present. "Thank you."

"But you're not going to agree to go."

"I need to be here for the walk with the cadaver dogs." I take a sip from the glass in front of me. Warm white wine is really an acquired taste. And not a good one. "And also, I think if he honestly wanted me, he would just follow us wherever we went."

Noah frowns. "You're probably safer with the cops sitting out front."

"True. And I haven't run from him yet. I don't want to start now. The house security system is solid. All of the doors and windows have locks on them. And Auggie will let me know if anyone is sneaking around," I say. "There's still no evidence to suggest Ryan is hanging around here. For all we know, he could have headed straight for the coast, stolen or bought a sailboat, and already be out to sea."

"You don't believe that."

"I don't know what to believe. He actually did used to talk about how his dad would take him sailing when he was little. But that's beside the point. What I do know for certain is that asshole doesn't get to tell me how to live."

"Do you have a gun in the house?"

I shake my head. "No. I hate them."

"You might want to think about changing your mind." Noah

sits back in his chair and gives me a long look. He seems calm on the surface. Though there's an intensity to his gaze. Something out of the ordinary. "Okay. We stay put."

We sit in silence for a moment. Then I say, "It might be a good idea for us to put some distance between us for a few days. Just to be safe."

"Sid." And he smiles. The man actually smiles. "I was wondering how long it would take you to try this. Hate to say it, but you can be a little predictable when it comes to my safety."

"Noah, be reasonable. He was so mad that time on the phone when he heard your voice. Just completely lost his shit. I'm not saying it would be permanent. But giving each other a little space while this is happening would probably be smart."

He just watches me.

"You're not going to fall for my bullshit," I say finally.

"I'm really not, but I appreciate you trying. Baby, that asshole doesn't get to tell me how to live my life either."

I rest my hand on my chin. He has a valid point. I would know since I just used it and all.

"It was a good speech, though."

"Thanks," I mumble. "This is all very stressful. There's a big old tub upstairs that takes forever to fill. Want to take a bath with me?"

"I would love to take a bath with you."

Come morning, there was no more police car. Ryan had been sighted seven hours away outside of Toronto. I can't remember him ever saying he had any connection to the city. The urge to get as far away as possible might solely be what's dictating his movements. Who knows?

He didn't care about me after all. What a fucking relief. Noah went to work, and things went back to normal. Or my personal version of the everyday mundane. One where a cop car cruises past a couple of times a day and my neighbors wonder if I'm a homicidal axe murderer or something. But every neighborhood has that one person they all talk about.

I make myself an extra strong cup of coffee after a crappy night's sleep. Tree limbs brushing against the side of the house was him climbing up the stairs. The wind rattling a window was him picking the lock. And on and on it went all night long.

I thought of going out and spending some quality time with my punching bag. Though the idea of Noah waking to find me missing put a stop to that. And I wasn't going to wake him to tell him when it'd taken him so long to settle. At around four in the morning, I finally fell asleep. Then being roused by the alarm just a few hours later well and truly sucked.

> Me: I am texting you from the great beyond.

> Hana: Dammit. He got you, huh?

> Me: Got me good. I am so dead.

> Hana: Bummer.

> Muriel: I don't know how you two can joke about it.

> Me: It's either that or scream and cry.

> Hana: Muriel has been stress baking.

Muriel: I have rhubarb pie, maple cinnamon rolls, and some fudge that's setting.

Me: We need to get together and fall into a sugar coma. This is of the utmost importance.

Hana: Wonder what he was doing in Toronto.

Muriel: Putting as much distance between here and himself as possible.

Me: Yeah. That's my guess too.

Hana: Has anyone heard anything about the corrections officer?

Muriel: Nothing yet.

Me: I have a bad feeling.

Hana: I feel for her husband.

Muriel: Yes.

Me: Guess we just wait and see.

Normal life is sitting on my ass and doing hours of data entry. I delete any and all emails requesting a comment or asking for an interview. Including the one from a publisher asking me to write a book about my experiences. I don't know how to write a book. What a joke. Though I guess they would pair me with a ghostwriter or something.

There are already books out there by people like me. I'm not sure I have anything interesting to add to the conversation. And surviving my ex seems too raw right now. What with the threat of him hanging over my head so recently. However, the presence of people like him is not necessarily something that will be absent from society anytime soon.

There were almost three hundred known serial killers active in the country during the seventies. Those figures dropped significantly in the new century for a wide array of reasons. Such as advances in forensic science, incarceration rates, surveillance cameras, digital tracking, and so on. But there are still some out there.

I want to be more than a survivor or a victim. Though I do kind of wonder what it would be like to meet people like me. Ones who have gone through some wild shit and come out the other side. But that idea leads to leaving the house and meeting people and trying to make friends, which I am awful at. Just awful.

By midday I'm standing in the backyard with my third cup of extra-strength coffee. Auggie is busy doing his thing. And the sun is horribly, insistently bright. Just this big ball of fire in the sky. I should have worn my sunglasses.

"I'm going inside," I tell the dog. "You don't need me to watch while you do your thing. Scratch at the door when you're ready to come back in."

He seems vaguely disappointed. Like how dare I not want to stand there and watch the marvel that is him peeing. But soon enough, he returns to sniffing at something in the corner of the yard.

I head inside, through the kitchen and into the dining room. It takes a while to adjust to the dim light inside the house. And another moment to notice the thing sitting in the living room in the black leather and chrome armchair. What was once Grandma's favorite seat for watching TV.

Long blonde hair falls over unmoving shoulders and blank blood-red eyes stare straight ahead. There's no doubting she's dead. Maggie Young, the corrections officer, doesn't seem as calm and competent now. Just awfully, unnaturally still. And the marks on her throat are horrific and all too familiar. Suddenly, I'm locked inside my body. The terror is so intense I can't move.

Ryan smiles at me from where he sits at his ease on the sofa. "Hi, Sidney."

CHAPTER FIFTEEN

MY EX WAS ALWAYS A GOLDEN GOD. MUSCULAR, WITH A classically handsome face. People would watch as he walked by. He just exuded confidence and swagger. His short hair isn't as blonde as it used to be. Guess he's been seeing less of the sun these days. And his muscle mass has gone from lean and mean to overboard. Working out was apparently right up there with therapy and finding religion while he was incarcerated. What a reach it was to hope he'd take up a craft. Watercolors, or something low-key.

His prison uniform has been swapped for a pair of jeans and a striped henley with a pair of designer tennis shoes. He always loved brand names. A gray ball cap sits on the coffee table. There's a fresh scratch on his cheek, along with a sheen of sweat on his face. Strangling someone to death takes a good amount of effort.

"It's good to see you," he says. "How have you been?"

"Fine. You know…a few ups and downs."

"Can't believe you used the date of your mom's passing as your security code. And they say I am obsessed with dead things."

"That was a mistake," I agree. "Are we just going to ignore your latest victim here?"

He sets his ankle on the opposite knee. Great that he's so comfortable. "She served her purpose. It was time for her to go."

Watching Dianne die had left me numb. She had just attempted to kill me, after all, in the name of a man I truly, deeply hated. But having this woman's body displayed in my living room is making my skin crawl. That could of course also be due to the company I'm keeping. This is my home. My safe space. And he has invaded and contaminated it.

"She thought you loved her, didn't she?" I ask. "Her husband's going to be heartbroken."

He just grunts. And the disinterest is wild.

"So, where's Laura?"

"Sidney," he chides. "There's no need for you to be jealous. Just think of Laura as my PR person. Lots of money in death these days."

I don't know what to say.

"This is nice. Just you and me. A relief to finally be able to talk to you without worrying about anyone listening or reading what I wrote," he says with a happy sigh. "I had to be so fucking careful while I was in there."

"Don't worry. I understood all of your implied threats to me over the years just fine."

He laughs. But same as always, the mirth doesn't quite reach his eyes. He's a stone statue going through the motions and pretending to be human.

This situation is chillingly similar to my recurring nightmare. Stuck in the house with him, and there's no way to escape. Even with my self-defense training, his size and strength pose a challenge, not to mention his penchant for psychotic rage. Though he hasn't started hunting me…not yet. Nothing within my reach would be helpful protection. Of all the times for the dining room table to be clean. My short baseball bat is on the other side of the room by the door. And there are knives in the kitchen. Eight or nine feet from me. How far could I get before he'd be on me? Judging by the way he's watching me I doubt I'd get far.

My heart is beating double time. I try to slow my breathing and keep a clear head so I can remember my training. But my brain flashes back to him strangling me, and I can't quite shove down by body's panicked response.

Having him here is strange, though I can't say that I'm shocked to see him. There was a certain sense of inevitability to all of this. He and I facing off after all these years. The detective was right to think I might lure him in. He never could stay out of my life.

Months would go by with no word. No sign that he gave me a thought. Then, when I believed I might finally be free of him, a letter would arrive to remind me. He was still watching, still paying attention.

I am a toy he picks up and plays with now and then. And Ryan doesn't like to share his toys. But he sure does enjoy breaking them.

"Tell me about your boyfriend," he says. "Who is this Noah Allard I've been hearing so much about?"

"How do you know his name?"

"Come on, Sidney. I have other sources apart from Laura. And several of the articles about my mother's death mentioned his presence at the scene. Of course I know his name."

"Oh."

"Tell me about him," he says. Like this is just a friendly chat we're having. "Or I could just meet him. Your choice."

"We broke up."

He snorts. "Sidney…"

"It's the truth."

"Are you sure about that?"

"Yes." I put as much venom into the word as possible. "And it's your fault. He dumped me because he couldn't handle the constant fucking pressure. From the police and the media…all because of you."

For a moment he stares at me. Then his slow, creepy, horror movie smile reappears. "Hmm. Can't say I am sorry or surprised to hear it. And don't be in such a rush to put it all on me. You know full well you can be a difficult person to be around. Is it any wonder I had to find an outlet for my frustrations?"

"Are you seriously blaming being a serial killer on me?"

"I'm just saying you had a role to play in all of this. Not that I expect you to admit it. The capacity you have for denial…"

"You actually believe that, don't you? That I'm one of the reasons you chose to kill people."

"Like I said…you're not ready to be totally honest with yourself yet. I think your grandmother went way too easy on you when you were growing up. Treating you like such a poor little orphan."

"Fuck you, Ryan."

He taps his fingers on the top of the sofa. "This is what I'm talking about. You're still not ready to leave behind the victim mentality and embrace the possibilities of what you could be."

"Are you serious?" I ask with all the wonder. "How about you? Are you mad about Mommy?"

"Can you believe how badly she fucked up killing your cousin?" He shakes his head. "How hard is it to frame someone for murder? I mean, seriously. What a clusterfuck. Not watching long enough to make sure you were alone. Then being stupid enough to leave a cell phone data trail that led straight back to her."

"But you're not upset about how she died?"

"She wanted to go out with a bang, I guess." He cocks his head. "Did you expect me to cry?"

"No."

He grunts again.

"You're bleeding," I say, nodding to the scratch on his cheek.

He frowns and reaches for a tissue from the box on the coffee table. Then he carefully dabs at his face. My ex always had an ego. How he appeared mattered, and that hasn't changed. I am glad Maggie marked him, and I hope he's left with a scar. Even though the woman made some bad choices, she didn't deserve this. Perhaps I can empathize more easily with her since we were in similar situations. Both of us believing, for a time at least, in the pretty lies he told us. Which reminds me.

"You told me once that the scratches on your arms were from me during sex."

"And you believed me."

I cross my arms over my chest and hold on tight. "I was an idiot."

"Yeah. Those were the good old days." He looks me over. "Still can't believe you cut your hair."

"Why are you here, Ryan?"

He stands and I take a quick step back. One of the dining table chairs nudges me in the butt. His slow smile spreading across his face is the worst thing I've ever seen. "I don't want to hurt you, Sidney. But I will if you make a move."

"You don't want to hurt me?" I ask with disbelief.

"No. I don't."

"Do you really expect me to believe that?"

He just shrugs.

"So the night you got arrested when you tried to strangle me…that was just an accident? You slipped and your hands just somehow wound up wrapped around my throat?"

The manic grin returns. "I'd forgotten how funny you are."

"Great."

"This is going to be embarrassing to admit, but I panicked when they broke down the door. The idea that they were going to separate us was upsetting. That they would take you away from me."

"You make it sound like you own me."

"Don't I?" he asks, voice oh so sincere. "I like to think it's a mutual sort of thing. Don't you think we're perfect for each other?"

"No. Just no."

As soon as he gets close enough, I'm going to attack. Target his vulnerable spots: eyes, nose, throat, temples, jaw, solar plexus, groin, and knees. Doubtless he's thinking the same thing about me. How he wants to end me. But he seems so relaxed. His arms hang loose at his sides and the creepy-ass smile stays on his face. There's no need for him to wield a weapon. Two strong hands have worked for him just fine in the past.

"Let's see this study your cousin was talking about. I've been so curious about this." He nods in the study's direction. "Open the door and then step inside. Don't do anything stupid. Just because I don't want to hurt you doesn't mean I won't. Trust me when I tell you having your fingers broken one by one is not something you'd enjoy."

I walk slowly around the dining room table to the study door. And he follows a step or so behind me.

I turn the door handle and push it open. And he grabs a fistful of hair from the back of my head and holds on. His grip is good and tight, and it hurts. I consider reaching behind me to grab his wrist and then pivoting around to strike him, but that would mean it's game on. And I'm not sure this is the right moment to launch into an attack. Because I don't just mean to hurt the man. I want to kill him.

"Let's see what you've got here," he says, walking me toward the map on the wall. The one of all the nearby parks. Brightly colored pins mark the fifteen sites we've been targeting so far. We've searched them on foot without finding anything, but we're hoping the cadaver dogs can help us find the exact locations. He takes his time, leaning in close to inspect our work. "Looks like you've been trying to find my girls."

I'm quiet for a moment, then I say, "I don't think you have any girls. If there were, we would have found them. I think the reports of your being a serial killer are wildly overblown."

He bursts into laughter. "Do you really think I'm stupid enough to reveal my kills because you're playing to my ego?"

I shrug. "I just don't think you have any kills. Tell the truth. You lost your nerve after poor Briana Petersen, didn't you?"

"You don't know shit."

"I know you."

"The funny thing is, you found Avery," he says, moving several of the pins in my map around. "But you're way off on the others. Here they are, not that your little murder map will do you any good after I start the fire in here. Make sure all of your research is destroyed and my girls stay mine. And if you don't behave you'll be added to the list. Does that make you feel special?"

I keep my mouth shut. The more in control he thinks he is, the better. I am going to remain calm and wait for my moment.

"I knew it was indulgent of me to take you to visit them," he says. "I tried to take circuitous routes to throw you off a little. But I just couldn't resist the temptation to be near them, you know?"

My brows knit together in confusion. "Why did you take me to those places? Couldn't you bear to be near them on your own?"

"Because sharing them with you was special." His gaze roams around the rest of the room. The books on true crime etcetera. And all of the photos on the walls of us together and all the places we visited. "See…you've been thinking about me too. We're more alike than you want to admit."

"This isn't me sitting around reminiscing about how great things were between us. And I can assure you that we're nothing alike."

"I don't know. Putting up this many photos seems more than a little obsessive if I'm being honest. Like you might be fixated on me." He tightens the hold on my hair. "I mean let's face facts, this isn't normal. My therapist would have so much to say about this room, Sidney. He would go on and fucking on about what all of this means. Though it does kind of explain why that other guy didn't hang around. You really haven't moved on from me at all, have you?"

"I hate you."

"You were always so much fun. Anyone with half a brain would try to pacify me right now. But not you. Look at you seething, and not even smart enough to hide it," he says, still holding my hair with one hand and grabbing hold of my chin in a bruisingly hard grip with the other. "The hatred in your eyes is completely out of control. So much rage barely hidden below the surface. Right there underneath that soft pretty skin of yours. And you've always been this way…so angry at me and the world and everything. But then they say love and hate are two sides of the same coin, don't they?"

"What are you even talking about?"

"This is your chance, Sidney, to leave behind this bland boring as fuck life and come with me. Just admit that you want us to be together. I want to hear you say it."

"What the—"

"You're a killer too. I know you are. I can see it right there in your eyes."

"You don't know what the fuck you're talking about."

"Oh, don't I? So you're telling me you didn't get a rush from watching my mother die?"

"No!"

"Let's experiment, shall we?" He sets me free, releasing his hold on my hair and chin, and taking a step back. Then he takes another. And another. Leaving a free path to the open study door and the house beyond. His smile is as wide as can be and his eyes alight with some sick emotion. "What are you going to do, Sidney? Huh? What are you going to do?"

I don't answer him. Words would be a waste of energy. What I do instead is sprint toward the kitchen. This is the moment I've been waiting for. I am going to carve his heart out and end him for once and for all.

His hand reaches out for me, but too slowly. That's one of the problems with bulking up…you get strong…but all of the extra muscle mass slows you down. The knife block sits on the counter near the entry to the dining room. I couldn't have positioned it any better if I'd planned this. My fingers close tightly around the handle and yes. I am now armed. He reaches for my hair again, but it's not long enough for him to hold tight. Not when I have some momentum.

Auggie is barking and scratching at the door. Such a good dog. But there's no way for him to get in and lend his teeth. Just as well. I don't want to risk him getting hurt.

It doesn't take Ryan long to try again. This time he seizes a fistful of the back of my tee. There's no good way for me to escape him in such close quarters. But I don't want to get away from him now. Fuck no. I want to get in nice and close. His fist comes flying at me as I turn toward him, slamming into the middle of my face. Something cracks and warm wet blood gushes from my nose. For a second my vision darkens from the pain.

"Drop the knife, Sidney. Now."

And that's the one thing I am not going to do. This is not the first time I've been punched. I don't freeze up in shock. I can take it and keep standing. He reaches for the knife but nope. Not happening. I won't allow him to take it. He makes a grab, but I pull it back to my side.

"Fuck," he yelps as his fingers only find the sharp edge of the blade.

Nice to know I am not the only one bleeding. I surge forward and sink the point into his stomach. The noise he makes is so strange. Like I let the air out of him. His back arches and he rears back trying to escape my reach. Trying to protect his soft underbelly from me. When I lunge again, he's backed up just enough to avoid the blade. But blood is making the floor so slippery. Not even those designer-brand tennis shoes can help him now.

He loses traction and tumbles to the ground. And I follow, landing on top of him. Humans really are creatures of habit. Because instead of trying to take the knife from me, he does his usual. Strong hands wrap tightly around my neck as he tries to squeeze the life out of me. The pain in my neck is excruciating and it only gets worse with each gasping breath I try to take. But I treat his big buff body like a pincushion and his hold weakens as I plunge the blade into him, over and over again. The handle is slippery with blood and gore. And a pool of blood surrounds us. Splatter covers the kitchen cabinets, reaching halfway up the wall.

His hands fall from me as his mouth opens slackly. Guess he's going to go out like his mom, with those same bloody bubbles on his lips. Though I am going to enjoy watching him die far more than I did Dianne.

"See," he says in a weak voice with a sloppy smile, "you are a killer."

Hard to disagree with him, but I keep my mouth shut. He doesn't get another word from me. And once this moment is finished, as soon he takes his last breath, I will do my best to never think about him again.

"You wait…I bet you've got a taste for it now," he whispers.

Then he's as still as the body he left in the living room. His eyes staring up at me blankly.

The knife falls from my hand and clatters to the floor. I can't quite believe it. After all these years he's really dead. I am finally free of him.

"Baby," utters Noah, from where he stands in the doorway. So much shock in his gaze.

And yeah…I don't know what to say.

CHAPTER SIXTEEN

OAH GENTLY WIPES MY FACE CLEAN WITH A DAMP cloth. There's nothing he can do about the state of my clothes. Killing Ryan was a messy experience in the extreme. My broken nose is a dull throbbing sensation buried in the background of all the various thoughts and feelings. This is a lot. But then it should be a lot.

We're seated outside on the front steps. Getting out in the fresh air and away from the dead bodies and blood splatter seemed like a good idea. Auggie is much happier since we've been reunited. He doesn't seem to mind being my emotional support animal at all. Because I am patting him like my life depends on it—such a good boy.

"You called her?" I ask for probably not the first time. It's like my mind isn't accepting any new information. Guess I am in shock. Finding a dead body in your house and butchering your ex deserves big feelings.

"Detective Hahn is on her way," says Noah. "Give me your hands. Are you sure you don't want me to go find some painkillers?"

"I am okay for now. Thanks."

No one is paying us any attention. Not yet. The old couple across the street are working in their garden. And one of the college students at the share house reads a book on their front porch. What must it be like to live a quiet normal life? To have no part in murder and mayhem. One day I would sincerely like to know.

With painstaking care, Noah cleans Ryan's blood from me.

"I really killed him," I say with something close to wonder. Though guilt or horror might be more appropriate emotional responses. "I stabbed him so many times."

"Good. He needed killing. You probably saved a lot of lives today."

"Mm." I pause. "You don't have to be here…you don't have to be a part of this if you don't want to be."

"I was wondering when that was coming," he says with a small smile. "I'm not going anywhere. Now give me your other hand."

"Do you think we should be saving this as evidence?"

"He escaped prison and came here intending to kill you. His death was clearly self-defense," he says. "You're not sitting there with his blood on your skin a moment longer than necessary. But they're probably going to want what you're wearing. You want to come inside and find some other clothes?"

"I am not sure I can go back in there just yet."

"How about I go inside and find you something for you to put on?"

"Do you feel differently about me?" I blurt out. "It would be understandable. What you saw me do to him. You probably need time to think about it. I need time to think about it."

He rises to his feet, his expression serious. "No, I don't need time to think about it, and I don't feel differently. You did what you had to do. I am happy you defended yourself. I'm ecstatic that asshole can't hurt anyone else. Just wait here, okay?"

"He said I was like him. That I was angry at everything. He thought killing him would give me a taste for it."

"What do you think?"

"I don't want to hurt anyone else. But I really wanted to hurt him. And I don't even feel bad about it."

Noah just nods.

"When the chance came, I didn't hesitate, and I didn't stop until he was dead. I am not even sure I stopped then. Guess he might have been right about my anger levels. When it came to him, at least."

The sound of sirens draws ever nearer. Detective Hahn beats the patrol car by a couple of seconds with an ambulance close behind. No idea why the paramedics are rushing. There's no one alive inside who needs their aid. Just me and my broken nose. It won't be long before the media are here. But in the meantime, an assortment of curious neighbors come outside to watch the show.

Detective Hahn's gaze moves over me. "Are you injured, Miss Walsh?"

"My nose is broken. There are two bodies inside. Maggie Young is in the living room and Ryan is in the kitchen."

"And they're both dead," she confirms.

"Yes." I get to my feet. Too many emotions are running rampant through me to stay seated. "He'd already strangled Maggie by the time I came inside from the backyard. Then we fought and…"

"Okay."

"He showed me where the missing women are. Where they're buried. The pins in my map in the back room…he marked out the locations. Said he was going to burn the house down so it didn't matter because no one would ever know. But we have them. We can bring them home."

Detective Hahn's eyes widen slightly.

Noah's hand presses against my lower back. Just letting me know he's there and thank fuck for that.

"He can't hurt anyone else, and the women can be reunited with their families," I say. "It's finally over."

Detective Hahn raises her brows. "Sounds like you have quite the story to tell me."

I almost smile. But mostly I think I am just tired. So worn out I could sleep for a year. "Yeah."

CHAPTER SEVENTEEN

Three months later…

PEOPLE ARE WILD. TAKE FOR INSTANCE THE ONES WHO gate-crash funerals. Some do it for the drama of the occasion. The chance to dress up and attend an event. To feel all of those heightened emotions swirling around them. While others are there strictly for the free food. I hate funerals. But there's no way I would miss today. Not after the family invited us.

I tie my hair back (it's slowly growing longer) and put on a black pantsuit bought just for the occasion. It's cold as fuck outside. But I stand waiting by the roadside in my grey woolen coat. The late autumn breeze is bracing—reminding me it's good to be alive.

"Is it that girl's funeral today?" asks Mrs. Lawson from her yard.

"Avery Lauder. Yes."

"Sometimes you stabbing him nineteen times seems like showing too much restraint." She frowns. "I'll be praying for her family. For all of their families."

"That's good of you."

I'm not saying the neighborhood loves me now. There's still too much drama associated with my name for that. But any media or tourists who hang around making a nuisance of themselves are likely to receive a sermon from my neighbors. It makes me feel less isolated to know I'm no longer so much of an outsider. Not so much a pariah. Just famous for all the wrong reasons.

Muriel and Hana pull up in a bulky SUV. Today is the result of almost a decade of work on our part. It's a bittersweet sort of feeling. With the help of the map pins, all of Ryan's victims have been found. We've now moved on to searching for other women who have gone missing in the area. The victims of other crimes. Because sadly there will always be more.

"The first of four," says Muriel from behind the steering wheel. "What a day."

Hana sighs. "I am glad they released the body to the family, finally."

"I honestly thought it would take longer." I put on my seatbelt in in the backseat and off we go. "How did your date with the cheese maniac go?"

"He covered me in Cheez Whiz."

I snort.

"I'll take things I never wanted to know for five hundred," says Muriel.

"Wait." Hana's brows draw down. "Was that a disrespectful thing to say when we're on our way to a funeral?"

"No," I say. "We need to live. Too many lives get cut short. You never know how much time you have. And now I sound like a bumper sticker."

"Just maybe don't bring up the Cheez Whiz at the funeral," suggests Muriel.

Hana smiles. "Got it. Where would I be without you girls?"

"I don't want to ever find out," I say with a smile.

"Question time." Hana turns in her seat so she can easily see us both. "Would it be weird if I gave talks about our work? How we researched the places he might have hidden the bodies and what we've learned about the true crime community and so on? And how some of my study intersects with what we've been doing."

"Like at conventions and conferences?" asks Muriel.

"Yeah."

"No, it wouldn't be weird," I say. "If you want to talk about your experiences that's absolutely your right to."

Muriel nods. "Agreed."

I curl my hands into tight fists. "Talking about talking. A publisher approached me. One who actually sort of seems to get what we went through. Or at least is open to presenting a not-so-sensationalized view of things."

"You said you were never going to write a book," says Muriel with wide eyes. "What made you change your mind?"

"I don't know. Maybe all of the misinformation. He's dead and the missing women have been found. My name has finally been cleared. But some idiots are still trying to push conspiracy theories."

"Some idiots will always be trying to push conspiracy theories," says Hana wisely.

"Yeah," I agree. "But just once I think I would like to tell my side of things. Get my story out there so I can really feel like it's been put behind me, you know?"

"Then do it," says Muriel.

Hana turns back to me. "What does Noah say about it?"

"He wants whatever will help me sleep well at night."

"I thought he might come today."

I shake my head. "There'll be media there. Best not to have him in the pictures. And they had a big function happening at his work."

"What about you, Muriel?" asks Hana. "Not tempted to hit the talk circuit or write a book?"

She wrinkles her nose. "No. I think I'll leave all of that to you two and just get on with the work."

"Fair enough," I say with a smile.

CHAPTER EIGHTEEN

A year later…

"WHAT DO YOU THINK?" ASKS NOAH, JOINING ME ON the deck.

"That it's amazing."

"It really is, isn't it? I can picture us living here."

"Yeah. Me too."

He slides an arm around my neck as we both stare out at the water. The house is nothing less than a dream. Three bedrooms, two bathrooms, and uninterrupted views of Lake Champlain. Over a hundred years old but recently renovated. Surrounded by mature oak trees with enough distance between us and the neighbors for privacy. Which is important. All of this and it's within walking distance to a dog park. With the added bonus that no one has been killed here so far as we know. It makes a nice change from our current home.

Ryan was right about there being money in murder. It's how we can afford this house. My book will be out next year. Telling my side of the story…getting my point of view out there with the help of a ghostwriter…it wound up feeling like the best way to put the entire fucked-up experience behind me. To discuss it in depth once and then move on with my life. Guess Grace was right about me needing to talk about it after all. Half of the profits from the book are going to charities, so I can sleep at night.

Muriel still has no interest in talking to the press. I don't blame her. Though Hana is enjoying hitting the true crime conference circuit. The story of our search for the missing women deserves to be told. More awareness needs to be raised around this issue. How much damage my ex and people like him do to families and communities and society as a whole. And leaving it to the *Misled* documentary and podcast people didn't sit right with us. They tried to pivot after my ex's escape and death, but it didn't even remotely stop their bias from shining through.

There are still segments of the internet who think I killed Ryan and corrections officer Maggie Young for fun. That I revealed the location of the women's bodies I had also slain for the heck of it or something. Some people just love a conspiracy.

It will surprise approximately no one that Laura continues working hard to push this theory. She still turns up on media now and then to shed her pretty tears and bemoan the loss of her boyfriend. At least she's stayed the hell away from me. I am okay with her being scared of me now if it means no more stalking.

Noah moved in with me and Auggie once his rental was done. We flew to California at the end of last year so I could meet his family. And after a lot of discussion, we wound up deciding not to leave this corner of the world. Noah wanted to partner in the restaurant with Ivy. And we made peace with Jade once it became obvious to most everyone that I had nothing to do with the women going missing. Thank goodness.

But the point is Noah was happy with his move to Vermont

and the new life here with me. And when it comes down to it, I didn't really want to live in a different city than my friends. However, we are moving to the northern suburbs of the city for a change of scenery. It is time.

I was worried the old house would be hard to sell given its grisly history. Fortunately, the real estate market is moving fast right now, and I've already accepted an offer.

One thing that's continued to haunt me, however, is what Ryan said about me getting a taste for it. For killing other people. While he was wrong about the temptation to kill, he did awaken a hunger for getting justice. By any means necessary.

I knew that after the book mania quieted down, I'd help Murial with the hard work of finding out who killed those other missing women. And if I had the opportunity to take out another killer? It scared me to think just how easy it would be. But that was a moral dilemma for another day.

"Are we buying it or what?" asks Noah, pressing a kiss to my forehead.

"Yeah." I take hold of the hand hanging over my shoulder and smile. Him, the view of the water, and this house are all perfect. Just perfect. "I think we're going to be really happy here."

Continue reading for a sneak peek of

WILDFLOWERS:
An End of the World Romance

CHAPTER ONE

THURSDAY

"**G**OING SOMEWHERE?" ASKS A VOICE FROM OUT OF the dark.

I clutch my market bag to my chest. "Shit!"

"Didn't mean to scare you."

The smile won't sit straight on my face. Not that he can see it behind my mask. You would think going grocery shopping at nine at night in old jeans and an even older tee would be safe. Of all the times for the dude from across the street to acknowledge my existence.

I'm average height and weight, with my long brown hair up in a messy bun. And there he stands at well over six foot something, shoulders as wide as Montana, dark hair showing traces of gray and giving me daddy issues, along with a jawline sharp enough to make a runway model weep. *Shit.*

Which reminds me.

"You forgot your mask," I say.

"Sorry." He grimaces. "Promise I haven't had contact with anyone for days."

"Me neither."

"You haven't?"

"No. One of the many benefits of working remote."

Some tension in him eases at the news. Which is fair

enough. "I didn't think you'd been out," he says. "But that's good to hear."

I lean my ample ass against my Prius and stare at him, bemused. Because what an odd thing to say. But most everyone is stuck at home now. He must be keeping an eye on the street out of boredom or something.

It's rare for our neighborhood in Portland, Oregon, to be so quiet. However, traffic tonight is nonexistent. Besides the ambulance speeding past with its siren wailing. The Thai restaurant on the corner is sadly closed. Probably due to staff shortages. It sucks because papaya salad would go a long way toward fixing what's wrong with me. That being having just about run out of food. But the combination of seasonal allergies and some new strain of flu have made a mess of the city this week.

Hot neighbor constantly turns his head, glancing up and down the street. Just checking things out, apparently. He's much larger close up than I realized. Then he looks down at me, and I look up at him and…yeah. This situation is giving me such a weird vibe. Though I do find beautiful people stressful to deal with in general.

And when I get nervous, I babble.

"The world is so discombobulated right now. Do you know, I tried to get groceries delivered but everywhere was booked out? I couldn't find a single place. Most of their workers must be off sick. I know the government said to stay home as much as possible. But I'm sure you would agree that when a woman runs out of cake, drastic action must be taken. Some odds are just insurmountable, right? A step beyond what's humanly possible to endure. Okay. I better go get this done before the shops close." I reach for the door. "Nice to meet you."

"You didn't tell me your name."

"You didn't tell me yours."

He gives me this smile. The whole time we've been talking, he's had a hand behind his back. I don't even know why I notice, since it's just the way he's standing.

"Dean."

"Astrid."

"That's a pretty name."

"Thank you." I open the car door. "See you later, Dean."

Guess I shouldn't have turned my back on him. But then, I didn't expect him to attack. Stupid me.

I catch movement out of the corner of my eye. His arms come swiftly around me from behind. My mask is pushed aside and something covers my mouth and nose. A cloth that's been doused in some chemical. It smells sort of sweet.

I scratch and kick as my mind spins in dizzy circles. But it all happens so fast, and the world goes dark.

FRIDAY

I wake up on a mattress on the floor. Nothing hurts. That's the main thing. And my clothes seem to be untouched, only my shoes and mask are missing.

The man sitting on the other side of the room says, "Drink some water. You'll feel better."

My mind is a mess. I don't know whether to be terrified, furious, or what. More information is needed.

On the mattress is a clean white sheet along with a

pillow, a padded quilt, and a warm gray woolen blanket. And on the floor sits a worn Persian rug in shades of red. The walls are bare brick, the low ceiling wooden, and the only window I can see is high and narrow and covered in some sort of thick, dark padding. Which means shouting for help is probably a waste of time. This must be the bottom level of his bungalow. Which is reason enough to lose my shit in a variety of ways.

But add the fact that I am sitting inside a makeshift cage, a prison for all intents and purposes, and I can't stop my hands from shaking. Like actual solid metal bars cut across the space between us.

"What the fuck, Dean?"

He nods to the bottle of water waiting beside the bed.

I sit up slowly and reach for it. The seal seems to be intact. But what do I know?

"I haven't tampered with it," he says. "It's safe to drink."

Our staring competition lasts half a minute or so. Though conflict may not be the answer to this particular problem. My current position isn't exactly one of strength, what with me sitting in an enclosure. Seems spending all of those hours watching cute animal videos and contouring tutorials instead of learning negotiation tactics and tips and tricks from escape artists might have been a mistake.

I take the top off the bottle and sip cautiously. It doesn't taste any different. And I am indeed thirsty. "What did you drug me with?"

"Chloroform. Thought you'd only be out for a while, but you slept the whole night. Must have been tired."

Iron fencing divides the room down the middle. His side

has a large TV, a plaid sofa, a punching bag, a bunch of storage boxes, and, most importantly—stairs leading up to the outside world and freedom. My side has a mattress and access to a small bathroom.

He's placed the bars horizontally. It must have been the best way for the sections of fencing to fill the space. Then he welded the panels together. And while it may not be pretty, it will keep me here just fine. One piece of the fence is held in place with thick lengths of chain and padlocks to work as a door.

I nod at the wall of iron. "I take it this used to be your back fence?"

"Yeah. The neighbors aren't happy." Shadows linger beneath his eyes and stubble lines his jaw. Seems the asshole needs a nap and a shave. "I want to make a deal with you."

"Do I have a choice?"

"No."

"Shitty deal. Why are you doing this?"

"It's complicated. But I'm not going to hurt you," he says. "You won't come to any harm while you're with me."

"Beside the harms of abducting and imprisoning me?"

"Yes."

The urge to scream and start throwing things is immense. But I take a breath and hold my shit together. Just. "You promise you won't touch me or make me do anything?"

"That's right. You have my word. But I *am* going to insist on the pleasure of your company for a while."

"Why?"

He picks up the remote and the TV comes to life. The news channel is running the same reports as yesterday. Photos of a crowded hospital in Beijing. Sick children in Cairo with mucus running down their faces. But it's the dead body lying out on the street in Brisbane and a mass grave in Prague that really get to me.

I swallow hard. "My mother thinks the pictures will turn out to be AI or something."

"What do you think?"

"Pretty sure Reuters doesn't print fake news, and that's where I first saw them. But it's not going to get that bad here. We've been forewarned. We have masks and stuff."

"Masks are great. But they only filter out particles bigger than fifteen microns. They won't touch this virus."

"Well, they're working on a vaccine."

"They are. But that sort of thing takes time."

"Time you don't think we have."

His jaw shifts. "No."

"I believe that we do. This is going to be just like the last pandemic. Fucking awful, but nothing like what you're talking about. You need to let me go, Dean. Please."

"I'm glad you have hope," he says. "But I'm sorry, Astrid. You're staying in that cage where I know you'll be safe."

"What do you care if I'm safe or not?"

"Because I do."

"That makes no sense." My whole body starts to shake. Not good. "Last night was the first time we've talked. We're veritable strangers, and you built me a prison cell in your basement."

"You're welcome." His gaze narrows on me. "Just breathe, Astrid. It's going to be okay. No one's going to hurt you, I promise."

"You have to let me out of here. And what happens if you're wrong about the virus?"

"You go free, and I go to jail," he says matter-of-factly.

I can't help but scoff. Though it sounds like more of a choked sob than anything. My want to scream and rage and cry at him, versus the need to stay calm and be rational and to try and talk my way out of this. Though I have a feeling I'm fighting a losing battle. There's so much fear and frustration inside of me. "Are you saying you'll open my cage door and then, what…just hand yourself over to the cops?"

He crosses his arms. Angry red lines are visible from where I scratched him last night. "I might try making it to the border. But yes, I will just open your cage door once I know you're going to be safe."

Deep, even breaths. Passing out in a panic isn't going to help. I need to choose my words with care and talk him into setting me free. Get him to see me as a person with my own wants and rights and needs, etcetera. "How long do I have to stay here? When will you admit that you made a mistake?"

"You want a time frame?"

"Yes, please."

"I don't know," he says. "Say a fortnight to be safe."

"You want me to sit in this cage for two weeks?"

"Think about it. We're probably going to know what's going on a hell of a lot sooner. The first time anyone heard of this virus was some vague reports from Europe and Asia on Saturday. But by Sunday, it was already here and circulating amongst the general population. Forget quarantine measures failing. We never even had a chance to implement them," he says in a clear, concise voice. "As for the incubation period—you have someone picking a friend up from the airport Sunday afternoon and dying early Monday morning. There were underlying conditions in that case…but still. Others have reported a couple of days between first experiencing symptoms and succumbing to the virus."

"I know all of this."

He nods. "Good. That's good. Let me tell you something you might *not* know. The survival rate is zero, the communicability rate is through the roof, and the current death toll is millions more than we're being told."

"Oh, come on. You don't think that all sounds a little paranoid? I know there are a lot of conflicting reports on social media. But how would they hide that kind of thing from us?"

"By shutting down the schools yesterday and telling us to stay home and stay safe," he says. "Finding cause to block the largest social media site for the spread of news and information at the start of the week wouldn't have hurt either. And this isn't exactly the first time the government has lied to us about something."

"Okay. Why are they doing it?"

"To avoid people panicking."

"Where are you getting your information from?"

"I spent some time in the Marines. Just long enough to get shipped out, blown up, and discharged," he says with a rueful smile.

"So you have cause to hate the government."

"Doesn't everybody these days?" he asks. "But the point is, I still have friends that are active in those circles. One of them has been working for a private firm. They've got her moving people around for the CDC and evacuating government officials from Washington. That sort of thing."

"Washington?" I cock my head. "But their figures are low. They're meant to be doing great with social distancing and hand washing."

"The inner-city hospitals are full and they're about to run out of body bags. Then they'll start running out of doctors. Washington has such a transient and social population. All of those important people, flying around the world and having meetings. And it hasn't even been a week since we first heard of this thing."

"I'm just supposed to take your word for this?"

He nods at the TV. "They're not going to be able to hide the truth for much longer. Not with things going the way they are…"

"I have another question." I sit up straight and take a deep breath. "Have you ever done anything like this before?"

"No. My worst crimes before this were some speeding tickets and a bar fight in Boulder, Colorado. Which I didn't start, by the way."

"And does your friend know what you're doing to me?"

"She does not."

"Why me, Dean?" My hand itches to slap him. Not that it would help a thing. "Why am I important to you?"

He doesn't answer for a moment. "I have clear line of sight to your apartment door from my living room window, and…"

"You've been watching me?"

His jaw shifts, but he doesn't say a word. What an asshole.

"For how long?"

"Guess it's been a while now," answers my stalker. "The

thing is, your trip out last night would have killed you. I *had* to stop you. But I would have had to do something sooner rather than later. Couldn't risk someone knocking on your door for whatever reason. Or you rushing off to help a sick friend or family member who could be contagious."

I shake my head. There's no talking him out of this delusion, however. "Can I have my phone?"

"Let's talk about that later."

"How high exactly is the mortality rate? Do you even know or are you just guessing?"

He frowns. And I mean, he really puts his whole heart and soul into the furrows happening on his high forehead. Then eventually, he says, "My friend was working close protection for a top government epidemiologist the first few days when all of this started. They seemed to think we're looking at ninety-nine percent of the population. Anything around those levels is Armageddon."

My mouth opens, but nothing comes out. Not for a while. "You don't really believe that. Come on. I watch the History channel, and not even the bubonic plague did those sorts of numbers. Not even close."

He just watches me.

"Dean, this is so wrong. Please. You have to let me out."

He stands tall and stretches. The man is all hard, lean muscle. And he sure would look pretty with my hands wrapped around his thick neck. "I'm sorry, but I'm not going to do that. You may as well get comfortable."

And this is when I officially lose my shit. "Let me out of here, you motherfucking asshole! You kidnapping cunt! Open this fucking cage right now. How dare you fucking drug me and lock me up in here, you deluded dickhead!"

But he doesn't even hang around to hear my rant. His face blanks and up the stairs he goes, leaving me to scream my abuse to no one.

To continue reading, finds links to purchase below:

PURCHASE KYLIE SCOTT'S OTHER BOOKS

Wildflowers

Because the Night

Text Appeal

The Last Days of Lilah Goodluck

End of Story
Beginning of the End (Prequel Novella)

Famous in a Small Town

THE WEST HOLLYWOOD SERIES
Fake

Love Under Quarantine

The Rich Boy

Lies

THE LARSEN BROTHERS SERIES
Repeat
Pause

It Seemed Like a Good Idea at the Time

Trust

THE DIVE BAR SERIES
Dirty
Twist
Chaser

THE STAGE DIVE SERIES
Lick
Play
Lead
Deep
Strong: A Stage Dive Novella

THE FLESH SERIES
Flesh
Skin
Flesh Series Novellas

Heart's a Mess

Colonist's Wife

ABOUT KYLIE SCOTT

Kylie is a *New York Times*, *Wall Street Journal*, and *USA Today* best-selling, Audie Award winning author. She has sold over 2,000,000 books and was voted Australian Romance Writer of the year four times by the Australian Romance Reader's Association. Her books have been translated into sixteen different languages. She is based in Queensland, Australia; living and working on land traditionally owned by the Jagera people.

www.kyliescott.com
Facebook: www.facebook.com/kyliescottwriter
Instagram: www.instagram.com/kylie_scott_books
Pinterest: www.pinterest.com/kyliescottbooks
BookBub: www.bookbub.com/authors/kylie-scott

To learn about exclusive content, my upcoming releases and giveaways, join my newsletter: kyliescott.com/subscribe

www.ingramcontent.com/pod-product-compliance
Lightning Source LLC
Chambersburg PA
CBHW020507120726
47904CB00003B/738